Forever and a Day

Jacquie Ream

ILLUSTRATED BY

Phyllis Emmert

BOOK PUBLISHERS NETWORK
Changing the World One Book at a Time

Book Publishers Network
P.O. Box 2256
Bothell • WA • 98041
Ph • 425-483-3040
www.bookpublishersnetwork.com

10 9 8 7 6 5 4 3 2 1

Printed in the United States of America

LCCN 2017943882
ISBN   978-1-945271-62-5

Artwork: Phyllis Emmert
Cover designer: Laura Zugzda
Page designer: Stephanie Martindale
Production: Melissa Vail Coffman

To my friend, Stephanie Martindale,
a woman of quiet faith and fortitude,
who knew how to laugh.

Friendship is the hardest thing in the world to explain. It's not something you learn in school. But if you haven't learned the meaning of friendship, you really haven't learned anything.

— Muhammad Ali

P_{reface}

If you have followed Fran, Dusty, Dean, and Annie in the Bully Dog Series, you might understand that I am saddened by their departure from my imagination. Fran will always make me smile to think of her as a young girl, bullied at school, who found her voice and stood up to the bullies. Dusty tugs at my heartstrings for she will always be torn asunder and reformed by the creative energy of an artist. Dean, the intellectual, always defining and redefining himself and the world, will struggle but ultimately win the wrestling match with his demons. And Annie, the saint and the sinner, is the synthesis of the friendships. These musketeers, these lifelong friends, these characters who embody courage, wit and grit, and faithfulness have stepped off the written page and into lives of their own.

I will leave them with some last measured thoughts. Fran, if Mother Teresa can have profound doubts about her faith every day and yet act full of faith, essentially becoming the "saint of skeptics," then so must we be faithful. Dusty, as Lord Byron put it succinctly about Childe Harold, i.e., himself, "the heart will break, yet brokenly live on." Dean, take Ray Bradbury's advice and "jump off cliffs all the time and build your wings on the way down." Annie, speak your truth, shout your truth, sing your truth, for as Buddha said, "Three things cannot long stay hidden: the sun, the moon, and the truth."

I wish you all a successful journey and hope that each one of you will drop me a line or two—I do not expect a novel!—in the ensuing years just so I know you are doing well as life goes on, through all the highs, the lows, and the mundane, for each one of us—you, me, and the reader.

Acknowledgements

As a writer, I appreciate technology and people that support the writing process with computers and readers. You might think it rude of me to list the technology first over the person, but without the computer, the typewriter, or the pen, I would have no manuscript to give my readers. I have replaced computers with upgrades, never so with my readers. I appreciate and feel most fortunate to have and to keep Nancy Adams, Heidi Clarke, Peggie Recker, my daughter, Brandy Ream, and my illustrator, Phyllis Emmert, as my circle of friends and family.

Chapter 1

Life's like a movie.
Write your own ending.
— Kermit the Frog

Cocooned in my quilt, I stay, reluctant to let go as the dream dissipates into pinpoints of sunshine. The smell of brewed coffee and the household stirring call me. I hear my father in the kitchen, dicing and humming, making a quiche, I hope. I stretch and inhale, breathing out slowly. Ah, to wake up with the whole day to laze; that's my idea of the first week of my summer vacation. My muscles ache, sore from a full forty-hour week of taking inventory at the Reed College bookstore. After finals, my brain cells were squeezed dry, and it felt good to stay an extra week to do mindless work and get paid for it. It is not as if I had to read all those books; I needed just to box them up and have Scott stack them.

My room looks the same as when I came home for Christmas, courtesy of my mother, with the Home for the Holidays banner still taped on the newly dusted bookshelf, which is really funny if you think of the two different versions of the same song by J. Cole and Perry Como. Of course, my mother would freak if she even heard J. Cole's lyrics. I thought about telling her but reconsidered, keeping it as my private little joke.

She doesn't find much humor in anything since Grandma came to live with us. Early-onset Alzheimer's now defines my once vibrant grandma who babbles and sighs a lot. I remember tenth grade is when I stopped calling her Granny because I didn't like the feel of the word on my tongue and it reminded me of the whole wolf imagery in *Little Red Riding Hood*, and she became Grandma. Mom and I once ticked off several breeds of dogs that Grandma might be and simultaneously cried out, "Poodle!"

I added, "Standard!"

Mom snapped her fingers and with a sly wink said, "Dyed blue!"

I leaned close. "But never rainbow!" I finished with a snort that made my mother chuckle.

My grandma: feisty, smart, strong-willed, and opinionated, the party girl—Democrat, that is. Used to be some lively arguments in this Republican household, but not anymore. The only politics discussed is the family kind, the dynamics of family members.

I sigh, asking myself if I sound like my grandma and wonder if she resents having her vitality ebb day by day. She used to practically prance, but now she uses a cane. It doesn't seem she really knows what is happening to her. I miss talking with her, especially when she would take my side and sway my mother over to my way of thinking. I can't help but resent the changes she has made in my life because she cannot function alone. My mother couldn't come with Dad to Parents' Night at college because she could not leave Grandma home alone. Really, couldn't Mom have made arrangements for a caretaker for just a couple of days?

I don't have to do anything today on this Saturday in May, and I might just stay in bed. Packing pillows behind my back so I can sit up, I look at the new quilt my mother made me for Christmas. It really is an awesome design of Galadriel, played by Cate Blanchett from *The Hobbit: An Unexpected Journey.* Mom has done a remarkable job detailing the sky and mountains in dark shades of blue and purple, the moon and clouds in white and cream and grays as a background to Galadriel in a gauzy, turquoise dress with sparkly white inset, a filigree headband, a shimmering aura over her, and an ethereal gaze somewhere over there in the far distance. Truly, my mother's work comforts; it's art not for its own sake but for mine. I should tell her how much I really love this quilt, but lately words clump inside my throat when I try to say anything nice to her. And there are times I feel as if I have to wave my hand in front of her face and speak slowly, "Hello! It's me! Are you listening? Can you spare a few minutes?"

Oh, well, let it go—my mantra lately. I feel so many changes in the people I love. Loved. Grandma with her addled brains. Dusty, my best friend, is married with a baby and husband and no time for anyone else in her life. Annie, my childhood friend, has been hospitalized with bulimia and anorexia. My longtime friend, Carol, moved to the Midwest. And Dean—always a river of sadness washes over my heart when I think of him not in my life—oh, well, let him go.

I scan the bookshelves. Should I choose a paperback? Or perhaps select a book on my reader? I have culled my mother's library for some surprising gems: Dorothy Parker, Doris Lessing, Virginia Woolf, and Margaret Atwood. On my e-reader, I have Zadie Smith, Dorothy Allison, Kelly Link, Jennifer Egan, Colette, and a few lightweight sci-fi books. But finally I decide from the stack of paperbacks next to my bed, *The Unbearable Lightness of Being* by Milan Kundera.

It's a complicated story, a lot about communism and political strife in Prague Spring, that period of Czechoslovak history in 1968. The plot line with the four major characters is intriguing and, like a jigsaw puzzle coming together, keeps my interest. Inside my head, I have done a little revision with the characters: Franz, an idealistic professor and lover of books, of course is me; Tereza, who sees herself and her body as disgusting and shameful is Annie; and for Dusty and Dean, I cannot make up my mind. Dusty is quirky like the dog, Karenin, not liking much change, and Dean has many attributes of Sabina, especially his lightness of being, but like Karenin, is a little confused about his identify. I go back and forth on who resembles which character the most, as they both have betrayed me.

There is a soft rap at the bedroom door, followed by my father's voice. "Fran? Are you awake?" He pushes the door open and pokes just his head inside. Reminds me of the joke about a camel asking his master to please let him just put his head inside the tent to get out of the sandstorm and eventually edges his whole body inside the tent forcing his master out.

"Hey! Popsicle, wassup?" I slide a bookmark into the book and close it. I can tell he is about to make a snide remark about my messy room, looking from my open suitcase still unpacked, clothing streaming out on all sides and stacks of books next to shoes and a shirt and jeans, to me, but he surprises me and doesn't.

"Popsicle is it? Now I'm a Franism?"

"Oh, no, no!" I wag a finger at him playfully. "There are no 'isms' for a Reedie—it's in the founding father's mission statement."

"I still don't know how I feel about that motto, young lady. 'Communism, atheism, and free love.'" He points to my gray t-shirt with the blue logo: a large circle, the seal of Reed College, with a three-point shield, a rose in each of the three corners, and along the inner border, the words "atheism" on top, "communism" on the right side, and "free love" on the left. Inside the shield in the middle is the school symbol, the griffin.

"You know, it was meant to be a slur upon the college because of the Red Scare after WWII. I think it was a brilliant coup—making it positive and all. It sure beats Foster's Comrades of the Quest. Sounds as if we're supposed to be knights errant on a medieval journey in some mythological story. Believe me, I have yet to meet a hero in armor on campus. The only 'knights' I've encountered have been the long hours after midnight studying."

"Well, I guess the only 'knights' you'll have here at home are long hours reading. You stayed up rather late last night—I assume reading."

I give him my "I'm *your* daughter" smile because he, too, will inevitably have to finish a chapter before he puts his book down for the night. I have tried to convince him to get an electronic reader, but he says he likes the heft of a good book. Now my mother, she reads e-books *and* goes to the library and second-hand book store, constantly exchanging her worn, sometimes yellowed-page books. Her favorites she buys in hard back. I have jested several times that every one she owns will be a collector's item that she can sell on eBay because there is no future for the printed version. She usually negates me with a shake of her head, as if the thought of it is too painful to consider.

Dad steps inside. He always looks nice, whether he is going to the office downtown or staying home. He has on khaki pants and a red plaid, short-sleeved shirt. He jangles my car keys and then puts them on my dresser on top of a stack of paperbacks. "I took your Camry in for an oil change this morning. Put some windshield fluid in and checked the antifreeze. Your tires look good." He leans on his elbow on the dresser, pushing aside a stack of books. "You've put some miles on it since Christmas."

"I'm a busy girl, Dad. I try to walk most places, only if I have the time. Freshman humanities is grueling and labor intensive. And, no, I don't read while I am driving, nor do I listen to audio books. I took to heart all those lectures you gave me when I first learned to drive." That made him smile; I knew it would.

"Got some coffee brewing and a soufflé hot out of the oven. If you are hungry, come have some, umm, brunch."

"Will do! Be there in a few!" I kick the covers off and stretch my legs over the bedside as my dad exits with a long look at the suitcase and a shake of his head.

I twist my arms and rotate my shoulders, glancing out the window at Puget Sound. Sunlight dapples on the calm, blue water. Then I see Grandma kneeling beside the George Best rose in her nightgown that gaps at the armholes, exposing her wrinkled, pendulous breast. I jump to my feet and fling open my bedroom door and holler. "Mom! Grandma's in the garden naked! Again!"

This is like the third time Grandma's done this strange thing of taking a parcel of food and burying it outside. It's not so bad if she's in the front yard because the fence hides her from the neighbors' prying eyes, but she is exposed in more ways than one on the water side.

At the slam of the sliding door, I retrace my steps to the window. My mom is racing towards Grandma with a robe streaming behind her like a maroon flag. The mothership comes in for a landing to recapture the errant podship, wrapping Grandma in the robe and her arms, lifting her to her feet. I can see her leaning close and talking to Grandma but can't tell if she is scolding her or what. They walk slowly, entwined together, into the house.

I pluck a pair of jeans from the pile of clothes, shake out a crinkled blue t-shirt, and pad barefoot out to the kitchen.

"Smells good, Daddo." He hands me a plate, and I snatch and munch on one of the four pieces of bacon, crispy and salty, a complement to the richness of the soufflé. I get my own coffee and offer to refill his cup.

He puts down the spatula encrusted with cheese and eggs beside the skillet on the stove and waves his hand. "No, enough for me today. Cutting back on the caffeine." He sighs. "Getting older is not for sissies."

I scoot out a chair and sit at the island in the middle of the kitchen. "You once told me you were never going to get old." I point my fork at him as I chew a mouthful. "'Forever Young' you sang all the time."

He places his hand over his heart. "Here, I am forever young!"

We smile at each other, both of us shaking our heads, which makes us burst out with snorty laughs.

Just then, my mother and Grandma come into the kitchen. Mom's expression is determined, yet she says softly, kindly, as she coaxes Grandma to sit down and have some breakfast, "Please, Mother." She slides a plate with a small heaping of soufflé and one piece of bacon. "Eat something. You've not had breakfast yet."

"Oh, my!" Grandma, enrobed in fluffy maroon chenille, leans back into the chair and claps her hands. "I think that all I do is eat!" She leans over to me and pats my arm. "I'll lose my girlish figure if I keep stuffing myself like a turkey and have to wear those awful, paisley caftans old ladies always putz around in!"

"Oh, Grandma!" I arch an eyebrow at her. "You'll never lose your style!"

"No," she sighs, smoothing her napkin on her lap, "just my mind." She looks up at my mother with a little, sad smile.

It is at this moment my heart pinches at the thought that someday I may have to take care of my mother. My father, too, will grow old, but it is odd that I cannot imagine myself aging or rather changing from being anything other than myself now at twenty. I haven't changed so much in my ideology as, say, Dusty; now married with a baby, she is no longer the Dusty that I knew in school. She has no time for the friends she had, no time but for the baby and Frank. And I am clueless about Annie, how she got to be bulimic. I miss her. I miss Dean. It just seemed that we would all be friends forever and that would be the one constant in all our lives. Now those summer days when we all worked together tending our neighbors' lawns are in some else's story.

I want to erase this moment, brush it gone from us, much like Grandma's motion of repeatedly wiping her hands down her napkin. Maybe she too would like to iron out the wrinkles of her mind. I grab her hand and hold it still. A thousand banal words scroll across my tongue, but finally I manage to say, "Dad made our brunch. It's quite delicious."

Grandma's hands are shaky as she brings a forkful of eggs to her mouth. Tiny bits of egg dribble onto the lapel of her robe. My mother has turned her back to us as she pours coffee into two mugs, twisting sideways to refill my father's cup that he accepts without complaint, and then faces us as she quietly places a mug beside Grandma's plate. For several minutes we are silent, and it feels strangely comforting to be here with my mother, father, and grandmother. The rustle of movement as Dad walks down the hall to his office breaks the spell. My mother sips her coffee loudly and then steps away from the island to begin loading dishes into the dishwasher. Grandma sighs, making a face at her plate. I swallow the last of my breakfast and get up to rinse my dishes, butt bumping my mother, and she reaches behind her to swat me playfully.

It's as if we are an old favorite jacket with its zipper come undone a bit; I'll just reach down and pull it up. *It's* all right, at least for now. *All* of us. At least for now.

My feet make a soft slap-slap on the hardwood floors as I walk into the den. I sit down on a padded folding chair at the card table where I am working on a puzzle, a Christmas present from Dean, of Gustav Klimt's *The Kiss*. I was putting ornaments on the six-foot Christmas tree and heard a car pull into the driveway, so I peeked out the living room window to see Dean stretch across the front seat of his red Nissan Versa to snag a box wrapped in sparkling reds and greens with a huge glittery bow. My mother looked quizzically at me as I left the room with a terse, "I'm not here."

I could hear them talking from the kitchen where I stood beside the refrigerator. Dean's last words to her, "Please give Fran this from me. Tell her I'll call later," as the door swooshed open and his "Merry Christmas, Mrs. Reed!" echoed throughout the house. I did not explained to her or anyone else what had torn us apart. How do you tell someone your heart has been shredded?

She stopped me with a hand on my arm. "Fran, I won't ask for the details, but obviously, something has happened between the two of you. I suspect I know what it may have been." She sighed heavily, quietly asking, "If I'm right, he told you he is gay?"

"Did everyone know but me?" I snapped, and then embarrassed by my outburst, I softened, "Yes, he did." I took a step away from her side but still with her hand attached to my arm, not letting me quite go. "I just don't want to have to deal with him."

She arched an eyebrow, speaking with her velvet-hammer voice. "You're a writer, Fran. How do you want your story with Dean to be? Are the characters over-idealized like in a fairy tale? Or just human, a little less than noble? Compassion, love, friendship all have a flip side. And we're all capable of being lovable and detestable, sometimes in the same instant."

She squeezed my arm before letting go with a parting remark, "You might consider his character development as a plot device that leads you to an alternative conclusion of what a relationship really is." She handed me the gift and left me alone with my thoughts.

What an ironic gift, the symbol of a kiss. I recall vividly the first time Dean kissed me, my first kiss. How his eye lashes tickled my cheek and the soft imprint of his lips on mine, how clean he smelled while my heart fluttered with elation. How right and true the moment was, and I just knew we were meant to be together. You can know these things, even when you're only thirteen. Of course, you may not know these things at nineteen or eighty.

I slip the last of the puzzle pieces into place and just stare at the picture of a man cradling his lover's upturned face in their entwined hands as he kisses her cheek. Her face is oddly static with her eyes closed and her unsmiling lips, almost as if she were asleep, except for her left hand clasping his and her shoulder pressed into his; her right hand is cinched claw-like over his shoulder and resting on his back. Her hands are more the focal point of the picture. Maybe on the one hand she wants his passion; on the other she doesn't.

I mosey over to the newly purchased roll-top oak desk that my mother found in an antique store and refinished. It gleams from the recently applied varnish with a sprinkling of dust on the edge. I swipe it clean with my index finger, wipe the dust on the leg of my jeans, and extract a black marker from a pigeon hole. I hover over the puzzle and then uncap the marker. The smell of ink is sharp as I make tiny tears seeping out the woman's eyes, dripping down the man's hand. The picture now is a symbol of my first and last kiss by my once-upon-a-time boyfriend.

It feels good to crumple the pieces apart and herd them into the large cardboard box, smacking the lid as it shuts all those thousands of pieces away in their dark container. Maybe the box is bigger to hold the pieces and all the symbolism. I wish I could put my life back together again as easily as I did the puzzle. I have been so intent on this inner dialogue that I did not hear the tip-tapping of my grandmother's cane as she came into the room.

"Oh! Grandma! You startled me!" I snip and instantly regret it. "Well, don't you look nice in that pantsuit!" She is wearing her going-out pantsuit, straight-legged pants, the jacket with large black buttons and intricate scrolls along the cuffs, and a multi-colored, patterned scarf, artfully knotted. She begins the process of settling down onto the cushion, gripping her cane with both hands as she swivels in a semi-circle before she lowers herself. She puts her cane on the arm of the couch, where it promptly clatters to the floor. I bend down, pick it up, and prop it against the wall before I sit beside her on the couch. "Teal is definitely your color. It brings out the green in your blue eyes."

She squints at me. "If you say so. Your mother is washing my robe."

Yes, I want to add, Mother does a lot of laundry these days. Without fail, Grandma spills some part of her meal, inevitably onto herself.

In her sassy way, Grandma sings, "You must remember this, a kiss is just a kiss, a sigh is just a sigh, the fundamental things apply, as time goes by."

I point to a photo album on her lap. "Show and tell?"

"Yes, that puzzle of yours made me think of a time long ago." She opens the book to a page with black-and-white photos and taps a picture of a beautiful young woman with long, flowing hair in a gingham dress, sitting on a blanket with a good-looking guy on her left and a woven picnic basket beside her on the right. "I was a pretty thing in my day, you better believe it!" She laughs and edges out a picture from behind the one of her. "I remember George." She holds out the picture for me to inspect. "Oh, he could kiss!"

George was not my grandfather's name. "What happened to George, Grandma?" I lean over to get a close-up of the handsome gent. "He certainly is good looking." Now this was getting interesting.

"Oh, he went off to war." She slides the picture back into its place behind the one of her.

"Did you ever see him again?" I am a little alarmed to see a wet streak down her cheek.

"Yes, I did. Your mother was just a babe in my arms when I ran into him coming out of Woolworth's. He had moved to the East Coast, Upper New York, I think. He said he had married and had children of his own. But funny thing, I thought at the time, he didn't wear a wedding band." She snapped the cover closed.

Grandma doesn't say anything for a brief moment; then she snags me with a direct look into my eyes. "What happened to your young man, Dean?"

I lean back into the couch with a shrug. "You know, the same old story. He found someone else, I guess."

"Really? He calls here, drops by, and I believe," she levels me with a fierce stare, "he has written to you. Probably does that thing with the phone, too." She wiggles her fingers in a comic imitation of typing.

"Texts." I squirm a bit under her scrutiny. "Yes, he does that, too."

"Then who jilted whom?"

"Grandma, I don't want to talk about it. Not yet. It's like my heart is torn, like a piece of fabric." I work my fingers up and down my legs, relishing the roughness of my jeans. "I'll get over it, I guess."

Grandma slips my hand into hers. "Sweetheart, tears can be dried," she reaches over with her free hand and touches my cheek. "Tears can be mended. He is not your intended." She claps our hands together hands and guffaws. "I'm a poet and didn't know it!"

I laugh out loud and take her hand, wiggling it as I used to do as a kid when I wanted her attention. "Grandma, get your needle and thread and sew the pieces of my heart back together again."

She pats my hand and says brusquely, "A broken heart heals with forgiveness." She brings our hands to her lips and plants a kiss on mine. "There are other true loves. You have to be open for the one that knows your name."

I don't reply.

As I watch her, I can see she is drifting again with that dreamy look that signals my grandma has stepped away from this reality. She begins a low, soft mumbling of names that I do not recognize, and I think she mistakes me for my mother when she tells me to wear the navy dress with lace inset when I get ready for my date.

I lean over and kiss her cheek. "Yes," I whisper, "it will make my eyes seem darker and more mysterious."

But she has not heard me or chooses not to answer as her eyelids flag and she slips into sleep. I disentangle my hand from hers and grab the blanket behind me. Carefully, I tuck it around her and push another pillow beneath her arm so she doesn't fall over.

I recall the picture of her lost love, George. The good-looking one that went away. I wonder if perhaps he lied to her, too. Maybe, just maybe, he was gay. "They don't always tell you the truth, Grandma," I whisper. "The ones that leave you."

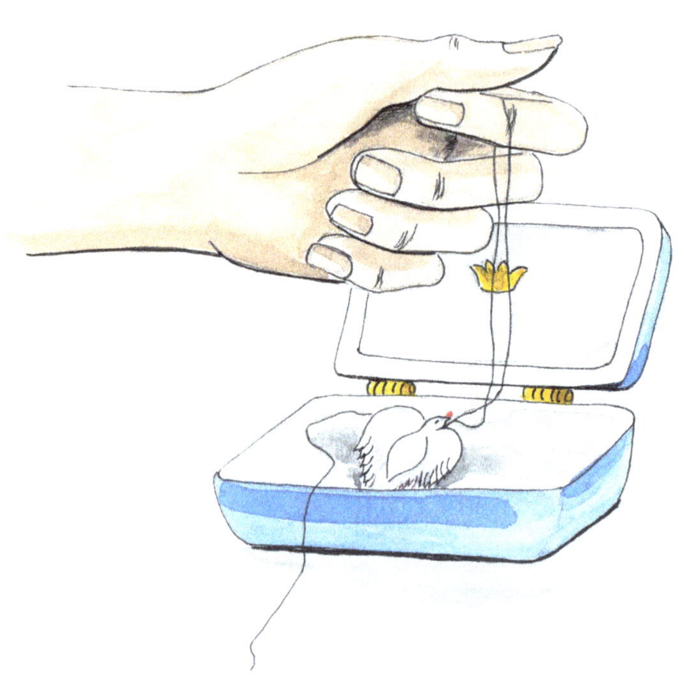

Chapter 2

The language of friendship

is not words but meanings.

— Henry David Thoreau

My cell sings Pink's "Just Give Me a Reason."

"Hello, Dusty! I'm so glad you called!"

Dusty's muffled voice is obscured by the whimpering of her baby boy in the background. "Just a sec," and I wait as she does whatever she has to do to quiet William.

"Can we get together? I could come to your house." She hesitates for a fraction too long, letting me know she does not want me at her house. "Or come on over here!"

I really am happy to hear her voice but at the same time have some trepidation about getting together. "Great! I'll see you and the little guy in an hour!"

I look around at the room as she might see it but decide that one way or the other, it does not matter if it's a mess. If we are still friends, then she wouldn't be bothered by it; if after we talk things over, we aren't friends, it won't matter what she thinks of me or my room. I run into my mother in the hallway with a basket of freshly laundered clothes and follow her into her bedroom.

"Hey, Mom," I grab the laundry basket from her, dump the clothes onto her bed and start folding and sorting. "Dusty and her kid are on their way over."

"Oh, that's great. The baby, William?" She picks up a stack of Grandma's underwear. "Isn't he about fourteen months?"

"Yeah, that sounds about right. March last year to May this year."

She stops at the doorway. "He's probably walking and babbling words. Eating solid foods, and exploring his environment. Don't be surprised if he's a handful. Toddlers can be very demanding."

I stand tall, holding out my index finger, as a professor might if addressing a classroom. "What goes on four feet in the morning, two feet at noon, and three feet in the evening?" I had to read Sophocles's *Oedipus the King* for humanities and do a paper on the riddle of the Sphinx.

Mom turns around and faces me, whispering, "Man."

But I know that we are both thinking of Grandma.

I take my stack of t-shirts and undies into my room, actually putting them away in a dresser drawer. As I push and arrange, a small box peeks out that is beneath an old sweatshirt. I know what is inside, and I know if open the box, it will mean a flood of painful memories. I scoop it up, tear off the brown wrapping, dropping the shipping carton onto the floor as I hold the blue velvet jewelry case in the palm of my hand, running my thumb over the softness of the fabric, the same color blue as the gown I wore for Dusty's wedding. The happiest moment of my life was when Dean gave me the necklace he had designed just for me. I finally open the box to look at the golden heart with a silver hand on the left side offering a bouquet of flowers inset with five gemstones and a silver dove coming to roost on the upper right side. The charm clasp is a small heart inscribed with the words, "4ever & a day" and a diamond embedded in the upper part of the ampersand. I just now notice the chain holder, the bail, is a gold fleur-de-lis. The bouquet with a ruby, sapphire, blue topaz, emerald, and citrine embedded in the flowers sparkles in the sunshine that streams in through my window. The broken chain snakes out of the bail and slips through my fingers, ticking against my hand ever so softly.

It was such a beautiful day, June 15, when Dusty and Frank got married. The blue of a cloudless Seattle sky can be so intense that it obliterates the memory of rainy, grey days. Everything about that day started perfectly with gorgeous sunshine that blessed the outdoor wedding ensemble at the South Seattle Community College Arboretum. Dusty was breathtaking in her bridal gown, not yet showing a baby bump. Frank is over six feet tall, and I must say he was stunning in a white tuxedo. Dusty planned her wedding down to the most amazing details; Dean released the doves, and I took care of the purple irises and mini calla lilies with sprigs of baby's breath for the bride's bouquet, the attendants, the groomsmen's boutonnières, and the centerpieces for the wedding tables. Dean and Fran, doves and flowers. Dean and I were standing alone in the Coenosium Rock Garden, and I had tilted my head to one side and said, "I think we might be the second nicest looking couple here."

Dean reached into the pocket of his tuxedo, took out the blue velvet box, and presented it, opened, to me.

All I could do was repeat, "Oh, my gosh! Oh, what a beautiful necklace!"

Dean had taken it out of the box and stepped behind me to fasten the clasp. Then he had kissed the nape of my neck and, in a low voice next to my ear, had said the words that made me wish we could freeze the moment for eternity. "Fran, we are soul mates, friends forever. I will love you forever and a day."

I would have turned around and put a lip lock on him right then and there, but the photographer appeared and waved for us to follow him for the bridal photo shoot in the Helen Sutton Rose Garden. Talk about a whirlwind of activity! I couldn't catch a moment with Dusty alone until the reception. But how odd it was. I was so excited to show her the necklace—"Look! Maybe we'll be the next ones to be married!" But her reaction when she looked over to Dean with a silent quizzical expression silenced me, and I had a flash of irritation with their friendship—as if they had a private conversation going on that excluded me. Before I could confront either of them about what *that* meant, Dusty's father interrupted, "The father of the bride requests this dance with his lovely daughter," extending his arm to escort her to the dance floor while Stevie Wonder crooned "Isn't She Lovely." Then the bride and groom were dancing to the Righteous Brothers, "Unchained Melody," Frank's choice, and the second song, Dusty's choice, Counting Crows, "Accidentally in Love." Typical Dusty humor.

Finally, after the bride and groom left, the guests dispersed, and we said our goodbyes to Annie, clearly enraptured with Jon, her fiancé, Dean and I walked hand in hand to his car. As we were driving, I took a deep breath and proposed to him. "We wouldn't have to get married right away, maybe after I graduate from Reed and you're done with your internship at the UW." So happy that I felt inflated with helium, I did not notice how quiet Dean was, quiet to the point it finally occurred to me he did not seem very happy. I touched his arm, asking him if everything was all right. He pulled into Rotary Viewpoint Park, and we sat there in silence for several minutes—I knew him so well, knew something was wrong, something he was trying to say without his bothersome stutter. My joy seeped away every silent minute.

He clasped my hand so hard that I shook our hands until his grip lightened up. "Fran, you know I love you and always will. You know that, don't you?"

It was then that I was not sure I knew much about anything. All sorts of bad scenarios ran through my mind: he had found someone else; he had a terminal disease; he was moving to Australia's outback, had enlisted in the military and was going to Iraq or going to somewhere far away to finish his medical studies.

"Just tell me what the problem is." I stared at him as if I could absorb him into my being. Dust motes danced in the sunshine streaming through the windshield.

"I'm gay." He said it without stuttering, looking directly into my eyes.

"Oh" was all I could reply. Then I wrenched my hand from his. How deep the pain was all through my body, as if the part of me that has no body but is the whole of me had shattered. "Oh."

All my hopes had been visualized in a jeweled dove, a future with the one I loved. The chain suddenly felt as if it was burning into my skin, and I reached for it and snapped it off, dropping it on the floor of the car, as the molten tears streamed down my face, dripping mascara onto the bodice of my formal. Dean had tried to talk to me, imploring me to look at him, but my last words to him were, "Take me home."

The next Monday a small package from Dean arrived by UPS. I stuffed it in this drawer without opening it. I had forgotten how truly beautiful the necklace is. The jewels twinkle, hard and transparent, like the absence of love; the ruby glitters, blood red, the color of anger.

Voices from the living room jar me out of my thoughts. I hastily put the necklace back into the box and stuff it underneath the sweatshirt I used to wear when Dean, Dusty, Annie, and I did lawn work for our summertime jobs.

As I scurry into the living room, I stop myself from rushing over to Dusty and embracing her. We stare, sizing each other up in the seconds of the silence. Dusty looks drawn, much older than her twenty years, but still she is so beautiful with her long, curly auburn hair framing her face that makes her green eyes luminous. She looks thinner in her skinny jeans and faded green tunic than when I last saw her, but I know her well, and I see the tension in her smile and shoulders, how she is both tired and edgy with nervous energy. The baby is fidgety and tugs at her hair. Dusty reaches up to dislodge his hand, and I glimpse a purple mark on her neck.

"Stoppit!" she snaps, shifting him from her shoulder to her hip.

Holding out my hands, inviting William into my arms, I take him and snuggle. He grabs my earlobe and tugs painfully. I clasp his pudgy fingers in mine and admonish him. "Oh, no! Bad boy!"

Dusty snatches him from my arms and soothes him. "It's okay, little man. Auntie Fran didn't mean to make you cry. All better, now? Yes, you'll be just fine. Auntie Fran is sorry, isn't she?"

Well, no. I'm not sorry at all. But I smile and tickle him, which seems to be the right thing to do. I'm thinking he not only looks like Frank but also exhibits similar behavior. My mom pops up beside me, all smiles and nurturing hands as she takes William the brat from Dusty.

"You girls go away and let me have this little guy to myself for a while."

Dusty has a silly seraphic smile. "Just for a few minutes, okay, William? You be a good boy for Mrs. Reed. Mommy will be right here in the other room talking with Fran, okay?" She offloads the strap of the diaper bag, placing the overstuffed polka-dot canvas bag on the couch. "There's his nap-time bottle, some Cheerios in a baggy, a sippy cup—if he wants a drink, give him water—diapers, wipes, and a couple of changes of clothes." She shakes out a matching polka-dot changing pad. "He gets fussy if he's wet. He's cruising, so beware!" Dusty looks as if she cannot be separated from her darling for more than a nanosecond. "Just let me know if you need me."

Did I just see my mom roll her eyes?

She waves us away. "Go on. Have some girl time."

"Come on." I pull on Dusty's arm. "Let's go to my room. Outta sight, outta mind."

She's reluctant to go but finally gives in to my insistent nodding toward one room away from her precious. I lead her into my room and close the door. We stand facing one another in the middle of the room.

"I never see you anymore."

"Fran, I have so much to do with the baby, housework, Frank's brother, Billy. My mom babysits all the time it seems. I just don't want to ask her for one more favor."

Should I point out that Dusty hasn't invited me over to her house? Really, couldn't we sit and chat between diaper changes? Instead, I say, "It seems like light years since I've seen you, Dusty! I've seen you four times since we graduated from high school—and three were events. Your wedding, your baby shower, the family baby viewing, and now. The only time I recognize you is on Facebook or when you text me. Your emails read like a mommy blog."

"That's what I am, Fran. I'm a mommy." She gives me a withering look. "Please, Fran, could you stop calling me Dusty?" She smiles tucking her head into her shoulder. "You guys are the only ones that call me Dusty. Frank thinks Elizabeth is a prettier name, and now that I am no longer a child, I should give that up—you know, be more womanly." She does her deprecating laugh, which annoys the stuffing out of me because I've seen her effect that pose around Frank. Of course, Frank would change that about her, too. Frank is turning out to be a lot like Dusty's father.

"What about Slinky? Do you ever see her? Did she marry that rat-tailed moron?"

"She went to Bryn Mawr. I talked to her on spring break. She's really turned into the feminist. She doesn't want children. Not that interested in getting married." Dusty breaks eye contact and shrugs. "I call her the man-slayer." Dusty twists the loose end of a tendril of her auburn hair, always a sign of anxiety. "I hope that she doesn't turn into a lesbian—Frank would go ballistic if I had anything to do with her then." Dusty shrugs again and twists her hair tighter. "What could be more feminine than motherhood? Frank never liked her much, so it's hard to hang out with her without irritating Frank."

This not-so-familiar Dusty-speak is irritating me. "Are you and Dean still best friends?"

"We email and text. I haven't seen him since William was born. Frank doesn't want William to be around Dean. I just don't have time to see *anyone* anymore."

"Dean's gay, not contagious." I give her a withering look.

We are in an eye lock-down. I want to break through to her, to the girl that I knew all through grade school and high school.

"No doubt about it, Dusty, you're fluent in baby speak, but what about you? You need something of your own, some area in your life that isn't Frank or William or household. You don't see your friends anymore. Have you been to see any plays, the symphony, the opera? You used to thrive on the theater arts. Your photography? Artwork? Music? Have you left that part of yourself behind, too?"

"Well, aren't you the," she scribes the air with her fingers doing quotes, "all-knowing, *omniscient*, college freshman who judges all with clarity," and then drops her hands. "Really, Fran, sometimes it isn't all about you."

"Maybe I should be more like you," I make quote marks, "the secret keeper." Then I add, "Only your secrets are visible."

She flinches, touching her neck, turning away from eye contact with me.

"Dusty, sorry, *Elizabeth*, you've lost all your color—you once sparkled, but now you're grey. How much are you going to let Frank take away from *you*?"

Her head snaps back, and we are face to face. "Don't make me choose between you and Frank, please, Fran."

This argument has shredded our friendship. Tattered and torn, the thin, tenuous threads that bind us thrum in the silence.

She fiddles with her hair, sweeping the long curly mane away from her face. I snag a coated elastic hair tie off the dresser.

"Here." I hand her the elastic band. "Get your hair out of the little man's grasp."

The bruise on her neck is not completely covered by makeup.

"Nice bruise on your neck."

Dusty swipes her hand across the offending blotch. "William did that."

"Awfully strong for a toddler." She knows that I know it was Frank. "Can't you see how Frank is isolating you from family and friends? Your friends, especially me, *know* who Dusty is— did you not have a blowout with your dad about him calling you Elizabeth because his new wife said Dusty was a childish name for a teenager and he thought you should drop it?" We are literally in each other's face. "Are you going to stop seeing your friends because Frank doesn't like us?"

"Can you *not* get the picture, Fran? I have responsibilities. I have a child. I have a husband. I have a household to maintain. I am a married woman and mother. I am not a college student who has the luxury of thinking about every little action that has a reaction, that all men and women should be intellectual equals, yada-yada-yada!"

"Frank is erasing you."

"Fran, the psychologist." She sighs. "You know, he let me name my son Dustin!"

"It's his middle name, Dusty. Throwing you a bone?" As there is a bone of contention between us to gnaw. "Can *I* call *him* Dusty?"

"No," she levels me with a look. "He is William. William is named after Frank's little brother. You know Billy and Frank are close. Frank wanted a namesake for Billy when he was in chemo for leukemia."

Suddenly, I am leveled by my pettiness. "Oh, Dusty, how is he?"

"He's in remission." She looks away from me, almost as if she is addressing someone far away. "He comes over after school and stays until his father picks him up after work. I seem to spend a lot of my days tending to the boys. That's why I don't get out and about very much."

"Couldn't we get together some evening and let Frank babysit?"

Dusty looks at me as if I've just proposed a trip to the moon.

I take her hand, lead her to the bed, and pull her down beside me. I shake our hands at the quilt and change the subject. "Look at this quilt. Isn't it awesome?"

Dusty pets it, clearly impressed. "Yes, it's more beautiful than the pictures you sent me."

"Oh, yeah. At Christmas time. I thought we were supposed to get together."

She shakes loose of me. "I was overwhelmed this year with all the family. I had Christmas Eve dinner and brunch Christmas morning. Frank's aunt and uncle stayed with us. I couldn't get away."

"Not even for a couple of hours?"

She sighs. "Fran, you've been at me constantly about this and that. Like a shark attack."

I pop up on my feet and face her. "You *knew*. You knew at your wedding that Dean had come out—he had told you he was gay. Why didn't you tell *me*?"

"I couldn't!" She puts her hands out to me as if begging me to understand. "I promised I wouldn't. He wanted to talk it over with you."

"It seems I was the only one that didn't know. I felt like a fool." I go over to my suitcase and pull out a gaudy velvet jester's hat. "I wore this for the Renn Fayre," I look pointedly at her, "which I invited you to come to in April because," I jerk the hat onto my head, "that's what I am. A fool."

"I couldn't come. I told you, Frank had to work overtime. I was breastfeeding William, and Frank didn't want me to take William that far from home." She looks imploringly at me. "Have you talked to Dean?"

"He texts and emails me. I don't answer." I sit beside her, the bells on the hat jingling in the silence. There is an ugly monster of betrayal between us, my friend and me.

"Oh, Fran, Fran. He loves you. Just not that way."

"Well. Maybe you can take a picture and send it to him. I'll smile." I flash her a cheesy, toothy grin, which I hope is grotesque.

"Fran, take off that goofy hat." Dusty snatches the hat off my head and throws it back into the suitcase.

She is clearly mad and ready to bolt. I feel that I am pushing her out of my life, and the thought sends a surge of panic all through me. "I've taken this too far, haven't I?"

Dusty softens a bit and nods but doesn't say anything.

I feel I should extend a peace offering. "I did a paper on Kenneth Burke, who argues that not only does man use symbols but also man makes and," I pause dramatically with a contrite look at her, "misuses symbols. I compared his work, *Language as Symbolic Action,* with a short story by Joyce Carol Oates, *A Brutal Murder in a Public Place.* It was considered very good."

"I bet it was. You were always good at writing." She blinks and stifles a yawn.

I can see she is exhausted. I stand and motion her to do the same as I pull back the quilt. "Lie down, Elizabeth. Mom and I will play with William while you take a nap."

"Oh, no I couldn't." But she is eyeing the pillow longingly.

I brush aside her objection. "Take your shoes off and relax. Seriously, there is something magical about this quilt, and you must experience it." I really want to tell her that I hope we are still friends and she is right about how everything does not revolve around my feelings or perceptions.

She slips off one shoe and then the other and curls up as I cover her. She murmurs, but I cannot understand all of her words. I think she says, "It's not secrets I keep, Fran; it's silence."

But when I turn around at the door to ask her what she said, she is already asleep.

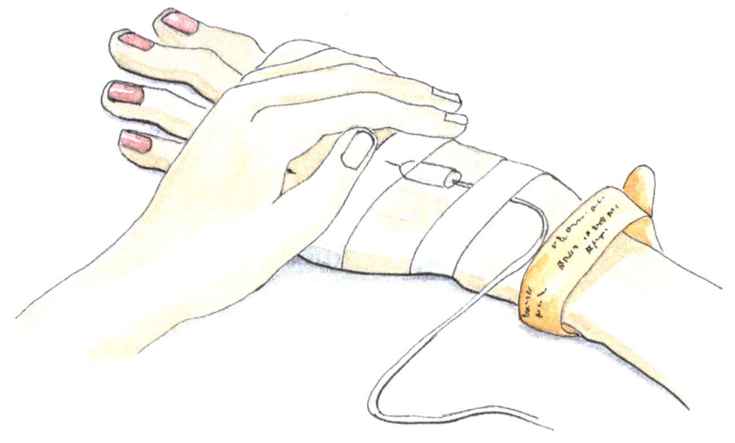

Chapter 3

Next time I see Dusty, I am home again for the summer. Dusty has come over to see me, and she looks more haggard than last time, so I do what I do best and put her down for a nap while my mother and I play with the no-longer-baby-but-toddler William. He laughs every time I hide his stuffed panda bear behind my back and then whip it out and jiggle it in his face. "Pop goes the panda!"

He snatches it from me and runs, well, toddles, over to my mother and, bottle clamped in his teeth, mumbles gibberish to her until she takes the panda, tosses it back to me. It seems we have been doing this routine for hours, but he has only been up from his nap for forty minutes. I am so thankful my mother does not mind changing diapers of this not-quite-potty-trained urchin and has so much patience with this dynamo.

"Mama!" he screeches, dropping his bottle, and scoots over to her, demanding to be picked up. Dusty swoops him into her arms and covers his face with loud smacking kisses, making him giggle until he hiccups.

For a moment, she looks radiant when she smiles and twirls with William in her outstretched arms. "Oh, Mommy had such a nice nap! And look at you having so much fun with Auntie Fran and Mrs. Reed. But we have to get home. Daddy will be wondering where we are." She has shifted her boy to one hip as she collects and stuffs his belongings back into the diaper bag.

I hand her an empty bottle. "You look great. I'm glad you got some rest." I wish I could convey to her how I worry about her, how I am afraid that sooner or later Frank will win and pull Dusty over to his side, the dark side.

She leans over and hugs me with one arm. "You were right about that magical quilt," she whispers, letting me go. "Mrs. Reed, I wish I would have told you last time, but I think your quilt is a masterpiece. Absolutely beautiful."

"Thank you, Elizabeth." She embraces Dusty and snuggles William. "Maybe William could call me Auntie T? He will have too hard of a time with Mrs. Reed. And I do wish you would call me Teresa."

Both Dusty and I burst out with a laugh, having the same thought at the same time, as when we were younger. "*Mother Teresa!*"

"Hey, Dust . . . Elizabeth," I sigh with a smile and she smiles back, "Annie had a relapse and is back in the hospital. I'm going to see her Friday. She called and said she can have visitors. I could pick you guys up, and we could go together."

"Yes!" She pauses and looks steadily at me. "My mother wants to babysit tomorrow—let's have lunch, just the two of us. I'm sure she'll watch William on Friday as well."

"Oh, that would be great!" I am surprised by this but unscramble my brains and remember a new place I want to try. "There is a deli up by your end of town. We could walk from your house."

"Okay. Billy leaves for summer camp for two weeks week. Perfect!"

She hesitates for a second, and I can tell she wants to ask me a favor; her eyes crinkle with her little smile when she is asking for a favor. "If we could go Friday in the morning, early like ten?"

"Works for me."

Dusty switches gears abruptly. "I've got to go. It's later than I thought."

"See you tomorrow." I am more worried for her than I was last year, as she can no longer hide the evidence of abuse that her bruises reveal.

But the conversation is not about her when we sit across from one another at lunch the next day. She pulls out a hand-bill and waves it at me. "Sign this! For posterity." She flicks a pen open and hands it to me. "I thought I would go into convulsions I laughed so hard! THIS is the best you've ever written! You are *absolutely* brilliant!"

That makes me blush. I scribble my name beneath the title. "Thanks. It really is a successful play. You wouldn't believe it—every one of the actors came to me and basically said, 'I am the one who must have this role!' Amazingly, everything about this play fell together *sooo* easily. You should have seen Leo Santos—Chulo?—he even had a mohawk that he dyed in colors of a bantam rooster. Oh, could he strut, too! There was a lot of ad-libbing that went on. Talk about a stage full of egos! I called them my basket of ego eggs."

We chorus in laughter.

When I can talk again without gasping, I go on. "Opening night was fantastic. Mom and Dad actually came. I got a bouquet of yellow and red roses—can you imagine? three dozen!—from an anonymous admirer, which I gave out to the cast and

Cast of Angry Chickens

Coqauvin .... Lynette Sayers

The Baster .... Scott Nicolson

Chulo .... Leonardo Santos

Rachel Tension .... Sakiko Anami

Monsieur Femur .... Wayne Rowe

Wingman ....Dan Blist

Pilon .... Bette Dryer

Feng Zihua .... Duyl Cheng

Thighman .... Randy Decatur

Chicken Tenders .... Morgan Peters

Mrs. Cooper .... Lailani Navarro

crew and everyone I knew." I leaned back against the booth. "Oh, how I wish you could have been there, Elizabeth!"

She meets my gaze. "I was, sort of. Dean was there. He sent me pictures from his iPhone." She pauses to watch my reaction as it dawns on me who sent the roses.

"Oh, of course. Yellow for friendship and red for love. How thoughtful of Dean." I pick at the salad on my plate. Dean would have flown from the East Coast to be at Reed for the play that night.

Dusty does an exaggerated and dramatic delivery with wide eyes and a big smile. "He is thoughtful, isn't he? Always has been, from the time we've known him in elementary school. A long, long time."

I sigh from the depths of my gut. "He sends me a box of Lucky Charms during finals week. No note, nothing but a small box of cereal."

She drops the playfulness in her voice and points a fork with a spinach leaf dangling off a tine at me. "How long, Fran, do you think he'll try to reach you? Right now you have it both ways—his attention and his desperate need to atone for hurting you. But he is human, and he will get tired of chasing you." She puts down the fork. "I know how hurt you were and that you felt betrayed, but can't you see beyond that?" She puts her hand out to stop my reply. "I am not going to get on your case every time I see you, but I wish you would reconsider how you treat him. If you can't be friends, then let him go."

"I know, I know!" I twist my napkin to shreds. "I still care about him. You cannot appreciate how much I worry about him, especially with all the awful things that happen in night-clubs and to the LGBT community."

Dusty folds her hands and leans over. "My grandmother used to quote the Bible verse from Matthew 6:34: 'Do not worry about tomorrow; tomorrow will take care of itself. Sufficient for a day is its own evil.' What good does all your worrying do if you won't speak to him?" She looks pointedly at me. "I don't think Dean goes to nightclubs. He stays very busy with all his extra credit classes and labs and internships, you know, that stuff that allows him to graduate sooner."

I lean over my plate and whisper fiercely, "I think about him all the time, really I do. I just don't know how to let go of my resentment. What do I do? Pretend that we are friends?"

"Well, you could start by answering his texts. You don't have to pretend to be friends; you two always were." She sighs and washes her eyes with her hands. "Do you remember when I felt abandoned by my father, unloved and discarded for his new wife, Sylvia? Did I ever tell you about the surreal dream I had about being in another reality and saving the life of a misbegotten foundling called Yugo and others like him who were left to die in the desert? A life saved by something as insignificant as a penny. I didn't want to leave the baby Monosapien that I cared so much for; but his mother loved him and got him back because I had a large part in making things happen for the better. But I had to choose to let him go." She clasps my hand. "It was so hard to leave." She swallows a sob, and I think she is back at that place she had dreamed. "Before I left their world of black, white, and grey, the sky turned into spectacular colors of the rainbow. I remember my mom asking me what is the color of love. I could tell her it is the colors of the rainbow."

"The rainbow? Really?" I smile at her as she catches the inference. "Actually the rainbow has been a symbol throughout the ages; rainbow flags date from sixteenth century Germany, even appearing in heraldry. Of course modern day, there is Apple's logo, post-apartheid South Africa, the rainbow nation, the Rainbow Coalitions, besides the LGBT and gay pride." I stop, acknowledging the meaning in her unblinking stare that I can obfuscate when I want to avoid an emotional truth. "Okay,

I get what you're trying to tell me. There are a thousand ways to express and represent love."

"Geez, Fran, you can overstate, can't you?" She stands. "Let's walk back to my house the long way, and I'll show you some awesome sculpture at a gallery nearby."

We walk and talk of modern art. There are glass sculptures of people that look so real I feel we are being watched and listened to by those we pass. And in some ways, these unreal people are less fragile than we are. As we leave the gallery, I turn to Dusty, indicating the building with a dip of my hand. "One day I will come here to see your exhibits."

"Maybe when I am eighty-two. If I don't have twenty kids living at home!" She stops short of her car, her hand hovering on the door handle. "You might see Dean Friday at the hospital." She leans close and lowers her voice, although no one else is around. "Don't throw away what you've had with Dean. Friendships are too valuable to let go." She waves to me, and I wave back, as she heads to her mother's house to pick William up. I leave and drive slowly home, wrapped in my thoughts that linger throughout the evening. At dinner, I don't talk a lot with my folks, and I go to bed early.

There is no magic in the quilt for me that night. I have disturbing dreams, mixed images of wingless birds caught in the thorns of a rosebush, and I fight desperately to wake, only to fall into another dreamscape where I am lost in a muddy corridor and then along a sandy shore with waves chasing me as I run for safety. I get up at six thirty, shower, and dress in time to say goodbye to my dad as he leaves for work.

"You were restless last night." My mother hands me a latte she has just made, probably for herself.

"Yeah. A bit anxious, I guess, about what to say to Annie."

She kisses me on the cheek as I go out the front door to my car and says, her voice like a benediction, "Tell her I send all my love and prayers for her."

Dusty is coming out the door as I drive up. She pops into the seat and slams the car door shut, snagging her seat belt and exclaiming, "Let's go!"

"Did you get the jewels and the money, too?" I hunch over the steering wheel and shift my eyes back and forth, as I accelerate. "The coppers will be here any minute!"

She bursts out laughing, relaxing into the back of the car seat. "What a morning! I won't go into details but suffice to say I'm glad to get away."

I tell her about my dreams.

"Kind of a double whammy today? I mean, Annie and Dean. It must be anxiety time for you—how's it all going to play out?" We wind around the narrow lanes of the underground garage of Swedish Hospital. She points at an empty parking stall.

Oh, yes, Dusty, yes, you are so right. Those layers and liars of emotions. I want it to be all right, a time for us when we are *all* all right. All of us friends as we were. I want Annie not to be broken, physically and psychologically; I want to be with Dean before he gives me the necklace. I want, want, and want. But here we are, so I ask, "Everything go okay last night with Frank?" I turn to her as I shut off the engine. "You weren't that late. You left at four."

She sweeps away my concern with a brush of her hand as she gets out of the car. "Yes, everything is fine. No big deal."

But her eyes, looking past me, reveal the lie. "Eleventh floor, room 221." She scurries to the elevators, smacks the up button, and then holds the door for me to catch up to her. We walk quietly down the hall.

I do not see Dean coming out of Annie's room, but Dusty does and grabs my arm and pulls me to stop. "I'll go in and spend a minute with Annie while you talk with Dean." She slips away into the room leaving me face to face with Dean.

I had forgotten how handsome he is—tall, lean, casual-professional in dark pants, light blue shirt, and shimmery tie of gold and blue, beautiful straight teeth complemented by his disarming smile.

"Hi," he tilts his head a bit, "how are you?"

Really, is it that simple? Just let it go, and let it come back together again?

I want to say, "Missing you," but I manage without choking up to reply, "Fine. I'm fine. I wish I didn't have to be here." Then realizing how that sounds, I say, "I mean Annie." I could feel the heat crawl along my neck, creep into my ears, and flush into my cheeks.

Dean reaches over and takes my hand and, without saying anything, lets me know everything is all right between us. "Be prepared for a shock. Annie is eighty-eight pounds." He leaves a space of silence. "You probably wouldn't recognize her if you saw her anywhere else."

He lets my hand go, and I feel the loss as we walk side by side into the room.

"Annie!" I gasp, frozen mid-step, unable to move forward. Propped by seven or more pillows, *little* Annie looks like a living mummy. Her shoulder blades jut out, sheathed by a thin layer of skin. Her hair hangs in brittle, thin strings. Thin. She is so thin and bony. I remember seeing mummies, Sylvester and Sylvia at Ye Olde Curiosity Shop on the waterfront, that had the same emaciated look. Her eyes, dark and lashless, are huge in her carved-out, fuzzy face. Is it a minute or an hour before I have my arms around her? "Annie, Annie," I croon, willing her back to life. The touch of her is awful, but I hold her for ever so long until I feel her shrink from my embrace.

"I look terrible, huh?"

I sit beside her on the bed.

"Funny thing is I still feel fat." She sneezes a small laugh. "You'd think it would be absolutely delightful to be told to eat."

I take her child-like hand in mine and, careful of the IV tubes and sensor cords, stroke from her wrist to fingertips. "You can beat this, Annie. I know you. I know you can. We're all here for you. My mother is praying for you, too. And she sends her love." I wish I had a cannon to lob prayer after prayer at her disease, make it disappear before she does.

Dusty is seated on the other side of the bed. She stands up, leans over, and touches Annie's protruding left shoulder blade. "Angel wings."

I am stunned. How can she? How dare she?

Annie begins to cry, whimper at first, and then full-on sobbing. "I don't *want* to die. I don't!"

Dean, the professional, the doctor, moves to the head of her bed. "No, you won't die, Annie. You'll get help from some very good therapists and doctors. Your parents are going to get you into a treatment center, and when you are strong enough to leave the hospital, you can be an outpatient there—I've done the research and the place and staff are fantastic. You will recover from this disease, Annie. And we'll be there all the way for you."

She swipes at her tears and nods without saying anything.

I want to ask her about her fiancé but am afraid to trigger any bad memories. As if she has read my thoughts, she blurts, "Jon says he won't marry me until I can wear a size ten. Oh, gads, I've never been larger than a size six!"

Annie, even in her bad-girl wild day, never did swear.

"Annie," I fake a jocular tone, "we'll all put on weight helping you get there—McD's, pizza, and—think—chocolate!" She loves chocolate, especially dark truffles from Armoire Chocolat.

A nurse, crisp and perky, bounds into the room with a tray of food. Red Jell-O wiggles in a white cup, and a chocolate chip cookie on a plate the size of Texas begs to be eaten. By the look on her face, Annie is clearly repulsed. Once, she might have been cute; now she is just plain ugly as she pushes away the tray.

"I'm tired. Thank you guys for coming to see me. Really."

"Annie," I solicit, "just a bite, a tiny bite of cookie. And one spoonful of Jell-O. That's all. Then we'll go and come back. Every day. Twice a day. But we're not going to let you go."

She looks at, really looks at, me until she sees me as her friend, someone who loves her. She looks at Dean and Dusty. Then she reaches out her skeletal hand and breaks a corner of the cookie off, brings it to her mouth, hesitates, and slides it between her teeth.

"Eat it, Annie," Dusty commands in her best motherly voice.

And Annie does. Then she takes a spoonful of Jell-O and sucks it down.

Dusty flings herself back into her chair with a dramatic "Do I have to do this every day?"

Annie nods.

I add, "Maybe twice a day." Gesturing with my thumb pointing to Dean, I ask gravely, "What does the doctor say?"

"I think," he leans close enough to kiss Annie on the forehead, "that the patient will make a complete recovery."

"Yes!" Annie cries out with a laugh. "Yes! I *will!*"

So, in a way, I get my wish to turn back the cover of time and have us all the way we were for just a brief moment, like a snapshot in a photo album. It feels so good, like when in the dream we all had been sitting together, but I forget the darker dream, the one about the thorns in the rosebush.

Dusty, Dean, and I link arms and skip down the hall to the elevators, just like the old days when we went to the Puyallup

Fair when we would do the chorus-line kick and sing, "Do the Puyallup!" But even that changed when we last went; the Puyallup Fair was renamed the Washington State Fair. And actually, it was the last year the three of us would ever be together as friends before Frank joined us. Nothing was ever the same again with Dusty and me or, for that matter, Dusty, Dean, and me. All the little things that happen are just one thing here, one thing there, but when you look at the larger picture, those onesies add up to the "should have seen it coming."

"Why don't we all go out to lunch?" I poke Dean on my left and Dusty on my right with an elbow.

Dean looks at his watch.

"Or brunch, if you must be so picky."

Dean makes a comical sad face. "I can't; I'm due at the lab. But I'll call you. Later?"

"All right, I'll answer my phone, even. Just for you." I snag his shirtsleeve. "And thanks for the roses opening night. I gave them away to the cast and crew, so you actually got a twofer."

"If you had saved the petals, you could have made potpourri. Then it would have been a threefer."

As we get into the elevator, Dean punches the fourth floor button.

Dusty purses her lips and shakes her head. "You two are something else." She uncrosses her arms as the elevator doors slide closed. "But I'm game."

Dean holds the door for our exit and then points down the hall. "The Market Cafe—awesome and cheap. Go for it." He waves as the doors close.

We sit at a small table. Dusty goes bonkers over the salad bar and fresh vegetables, and I love the grilled hamburger. We split a chocolate cake that is simply heavenly, all the while chatting about anything and everything but issues like her marriage, Annie's disease, or my relationship with Dean.

"Is there anyone in your life—man-kind, Fran?"

"Oh, yes, no, not really." I shrug, smiling. "Scott Nicolson, the Baster in *Angry Chickens*. I work with him at the bookshop."

"Is he attractive?"

"Yeah, he is. Little taller than I am, seriously blue eyes, and blondish hair, surfer-boy cut. Dresses neatly. He has asked me out for coffee. But you know, not like a date." I shrug again, maybe to get the idea of a boyfriend off my shoulders. "Not really that interested."

"You or him?" She leans on her elbows and looks at me pointedly. "A little trust issue maybe?"

"Maybe." I hurry on, to avoid the subject. "You think Annie's going to be all right? She looks . . . she looks like she's . . ."

"Nearly dead." Dusty straightens herself. "Really. I don't know. I guess all we can do is what we can do. Be her support and pray for her."

"Well, I know I can support her through friendship, but I don't know if my prayers make a difference."

"Fran, that's when you have to have faith. You have to believe that it matters, it all means something, even if you don't know."

"Trust issues. I have trust issues? Don't you?"

She looks at me hard, then leans closer, and lowers her voice, yet her fragmented words are vehement. "You don't think I know what Frank is doing? To me? Isolating me from my friends and family? All with threats and physical violence? I have no one I can trust. I cannot even confide in my mother for fear of Frankenstein. The endless arguments . . . always about something I have done that makes him mad. A wrong word or gesture can set Frank off in a tirade . . . or worse. I'm afraid of him. Afraid he will do more than break my wrist, leave bruises. I'm afraid he will hurt my son. Or even kill me. He blames me for ruining his chance at having a career as a professional baseball player. As if I am the only one that conceived a baby?" She sits upright, as if to change her life with the right attitude, the right words, a different tone of voice. "My, that sounds so dramatic! I still have a spark of hope that he will change. William adores him, what little he sees of him. I placate him as much as I can, hope he will realize that a loving family is worth more than his affairs."

Before I can say anything, she adds wistfully, "I envy you, Fran, envy your life, your independence, your education, and your future. But I have my faith."

She looks me over and shakes her head, veering into another topic. "I met Marcus, Dean's partner."

"What did you think of him? You have that funny look where you scrunch up your lip and nose when you don't like something."

"Oh, I like Marcus. I don't like the way Dean treats him sometimes. Dean can be pretty self-centered and demanding to get his way."

I am surprised to hear her criticize Dean, for she always maintained that he was one of the good guys. Then I realize she does not love or like him any less for his flaws. "Do you see them staying together?" With a pang I think maybe she can tell me that Dean really wants to go straight.

"Oh, like any relationship, they will have to work through their differences." She shags an eyebrow. "As we all do."

No! I want to shout, you cannot work through differences when there is abuse.

Dusty goes into her abrupt change mode. "Time to go. My mom has an appointment."

I think that's a lie, but I don't challenge her. My thoughts whirl in a thousand directions, but I know she has to leave Frank, and I must try to convince her.

We leave in my car. Her house is quiet, almost too quiet when we enter through the front door. Mrs. Conner greets us with a pulsing finger to her mouth. "Shh, he's finally asleep. How's Annie?" she whispers.

Dusty waves us into the kitchen. "She doesn't look good, but Dean thinks she'll be okay. She ate two," Dusty flips a *V* sign, "two bites—an itsy bit of cookie and a spoonful of Jell-O—and Dean just about broke out the champagne. But we can at least have hope."

Dusty gestures with splayed hands pumping to the espresso maker. "Can I make us all a latte on the Saeco Vienna Plus super-auto espresso machine, a present from my loving husband?"

I cannot say for sure that Mrs. Conner's expression hardened or that she visibly tensed when Dusty said "loving husband," but there was definitely a change in her demeanor, almost as if she recoiled at what the espresso maker symbolized.

"Oh, not for me. I'll leave you two girls to yourselves. I'm quite confident you can find trouble without me."

"Mom, thanks for today. I appreciate that."

"No, honey, I appreciate you letting me have time with my grandson. He's so adorable. I love him almost as much as I love you." She kisses Dusty resoundingly on the cheek and gives my arm a quick pat as she lets herself out the back door.

Dusty yawns, wiping her hands across her eyes. "A latte for me. You?"

"Are you sure you want coffee and not a nap?"

"Frank will be home soon. I'll go to bed early. Let's have a latte!"

There is no conversation during the whirring of the beans and steaming of the milk. Finally, in the lull when Dusty hands me my cup, I ask her. "You, Elizabeth, how are you? I am, quite *frankly* worried for you and about you."

"Well, quite *frankly*, it's not so good." She sips her coffee, puts the cup down, and adds two teaspoons of sugar. "His affairs don't bother me as much as his temper. He threatens to take William away if I leave him. And he's got the money to get a lawyer to do it, too. Believe me."

I would like to believe that I am surprised by her candid admission, but it all adds up. "You'll have to leave. You can't live like this—afraid to be, afraid from one day to the next. I'll help you. And you know Dean will."

She stirs her coffee longer than necessary, taps the spoon on the side of the cup, rinses it under the faucet, puts it in the dish rack. "It would be a consideration if I weren't pregnant."

Well, stun gun.

"And just when were you going to tell me?" bellows Frank looming large and angry at the doorway.

"Frank, please!" Dusty at once supplicates with her up-turned hands and scowls.

William wakes screaming, impelling Dusty to go to him, leaving Frank and me alone in a standoff.

"Oh, hello, Frank," I say in my best I'm-being-polite-and-you-are-not voice.

He takes a step inside the kitchen. "Don't you have a Communist Manifesto to read or a meeting at the Rainbow Club?"

"You make it a point to be pointless, don't you, Frank?"

Dusty flies in between us, patting screeching-owl William on the back as she turns first to Frank, "Why don't you grab a beer and go chill for a minute," then to me, "and I'll walk you to your car."

I start to protest, but she silences me with a look. We are outside when I turn and petition her, "Come with me, now. I'll take you to your mother's, my place, a motel. But don't stay here with him. You're not safe with him, especially like he is. Come on; get in the car."

"No, Fran, listen to me. I can't leave yet. Not right now, I'll be okay—Frank's fine. He'll calm down after he has a beer, and we'll talk things out. I'll call you. Tomorrow."

"No! Come with me—"

"I'm fine, Fran. Go on home. I'll talk to you tomorrow."

She turns and walks back into the house.

As they say, tomorrow never comes.

Chapter 4

*The bird a nest, the spider
a web, man friendship.*

— William Blake

The weather shifted from a balmy to a rainy morning. Mom and I went to the Home Depot and got Early Girl and Sweet 100 tomato plants, along with pansies and verbena to put with them in the prepared soil. We have a long discussion where the perennials will go—as accents along the borders of the vegetables or in pots on the deck. As the rain pelts us, we decide to line them up on the deck in their green pots and finish the project under more auspicious skies.

I have just finished texting Annie for the fourth time since I awoke at 7:30 a.m., sending her another funny e-card, this one with a little girl in tutu, upside down on the barre, obviously entangled as all the other girls are doing it right. The caption reads, "Get me outta here!" It was a running joke with us when were young girls in ballet class that I had exceptional talent for getting it backwards and Annie, ever graceful and focused, was the prima ballerina.

"CU afternoon. Bye."

I have just sent the text off when my cell rings. "Dusty! Is everything all right?"

"Fran," her voice is soft and scratchy, "I need to talk to you."

I am standing by the boot box, and I pop one shoe off with my foot and then the other. "Sure, want me to come over?"

"No, Fran, come to the hospital. Swedish. Room 1119, south wing."

"What happened?" My hands are shaking; I am so frightened.

"I lost the baby. Frank . . . he beat me up, Fran. Kicked me in the stomach." Her tiny voice becomes emboldened. "Did you mean it when you said you would help me leave him?"

"Yes, yes. I'll call Dean and tell him. We'll figure something out. Where is William?"

"My mom has him. The doctor is here. Bye."

My mom lays a hand on my arm. "What?"

"Dusty is in the hospital. She miscarried."

"I'll drive you. It would do no one any good for you to be in an accident because you are distracted."

"Oh, Mother, you can't leave Grandma. I'm fine. Really." Her hand lies warm on my arm. I lean over and kiss her cheek. "Thanks, anyway. I'll be extra careful, I promise."

I call Dean, tell him we have to get Dusty somewhere safe.

"She and William can stay with me. I'm alone for the week. But she'll need some money, Fran, to live on. I can help some, but honestly, I don't have much."

I ponder that for a moment. "My folks would, but then I'll have to tell the whole story. I'll ask her father to help out. I'll go by his place and ask him before I go to the hospital."

I sit in the car in front of the house where Dusty's father, his wife, Sylvia, and their eight-year-old daughter live, running my hands over, up and down the steering wheel for what seems an hour before I screw enough courage into my backbone to get out of the car, go to the front door, and knock.

Sylvia answers. "Fran! This is a surprise! Come in, please."

I know Dusty dislikes this woman, but my, she is gorgeous, impeccable in dress and makeup, and giving out nice vibes as she leads me to the living room.

"Can I get you coffee or tea?"

"Actually, I need to talk to Mr. Connor. It's really important." My hands are sweaty, and I can feel droplets running down my back. Dusty will disown me for sure if she finds out I've come here.

"He's out of town, Fran. He won't be home until a week from Thursday." She eyes me as if I might have drugs on me. "What is it, Fran? Talk to me. You're obviously upset and worried by the tension in your face and your fluttering hands. Is it Elizabeth?"

"Yes!" I fairly screech. "She's in the hospital." How am I going to make my case unless I tell the truth? "She miscarried because Frank kicked her. Dean and I are going to take her and William to a safe place, but she'll need money to live on, and we just don't have it. Do you think her father will give her some support?"

Sylvia, stunned, opens her mouth to say something, shuts her mouth, and looks at me for a moment before she says, "We didn't know Elizabeth was pregnant. Where's William?"

I take a deep breath and shake off my panic. "With Dusty's mom. I promised I'd get to the hospital right away to see Dusty." I glance at my watch, more out of nervousness and to break the intensity of eye contact with Sylvia because I really do not see the time.

"Wait here a minute. I'll be right back."

I catch a glimpse of Sophia through the opened door of her pink bedroom, sitting on her bed with a fluffy pink-and-blue cover. I see a beautiful child who will likely be a beautiful woman.

Sylvia comes back into the room with an envelope that she hands to me. "It's all I have for now, Fran. It'll tide Elizabeth over until her father gets home and we can figure out what is to be done."

"Oh, gosh, oh, thank you." It was a thousand dollars, if not more. "I don't know what to say."

"Tell Elizabeth it is from her father, not from me. We're not exactly buds."

She walks me to the door. "Drive safely, Fran. Please no texting or using your phone."

Do all mothers have a manual of cautionary lines for any occasion?

"I won't, I promise." I feel about twelve years old but strangely do not resent Sylvia's motherly advice because she seems so genuinely caring.

I get to the hospital fine. Even though the traffic was slow, it moved along, and I found a parking space on the third floor. I call my mother to let her know I'm safely there as I get into the elevator. However, I get lost and wind my way through corridor after corridor before I find the sky bridge and a sign that indicates the south wing.

Once there, I go through the door and stop and wait for the nurse to finish adjusting the bed. If it were not for the setting, Dusty might have been a model posing for a shoot. Her beautiful long auburn hair with copper highlights spreads over her shoulders and frames her face artfully. Her lips are slightly parted, and if she did not look so pale with an IV in her arm and a sensor on her finger for the monitor, I would have taken a picture of her. I should have.

Inching over to the chair beside her bed, I sit and wait. The nurse leaves with a smile and nod at me. Dusty does not look at me right away but twists a lock of her hair and then wets her lips. I can see the other side of her face has turned purple and green and she has a black eye.

"I lost the baby. A girl."

She is so calm, matter-of-fact that it takes a minute for me to respond. I swallow, but the words just stick in my throat. "I'm sorry," I croak.

"Fran, you said you would help me leave Frank." She turns and looks me straight in the eyes, still calm, matter-of-fact. "Will you?"

I straighten up, reach for her hand, and hold it. "Yes, I will. Dean will, too. I'll call him, and we'll get a plan. You won't leave the hospital with Frank; you'll leave with us."

"William, too."

"Of course. The both of you—we'll find you some place safe and make plans. Don't worry. By tomorrow, Dean and I will have a game plan. Have you called Dean?"

"No, just you."

"Don't say anything to Frank about this! Anything! No matter how tempted you might be to tell him, don't. Okay?"

"Yes, of course."

I am furiously texting Dean and trying to line my thoughts in some sort of order. "Where's William?" I remember asking her this in the phone call, but I need to say something other than blurt out that I went to see her father, who is on a trip. Does Dusty know that? Then she would know that Sylvia gave me money for her sake.

"My mother's. He's safe."

"What happened?" I whisper though I do not know why I am being secretive; my battered friend's face tells me what happened.

"He started yelling at me for not having dinner ready, then taunting me about being pregnant. William was crying, and Frank smacked him, told him to shut up. I snapped, slapped

Frank as hard as I could. He's bigger and stronger than I am. I lost."

We sit wrapped in the silence of our friendship, just being there with one another, until footsteps snag our attention. Frank comes into the room with a bouquet of at least four dozen white, pink, yellow, and red roses. The warmth drains out the room, and the silence is awkward. Frank looks at me and nods to the door, indicating I should leave. I sit and stare at him.

"Fran," he exaggerates his words, "if you wouldn't mind, I'd like to talk to Elizabeth. My wife. Alone."

"No." Though I thought of saying it, Dusty says it first. "She is going to stay right there until she wants to leave."

He shrugs, approaches her, offering her the roses. "I'm sorry, Elizabeth. Really, I am. About everything. Everything."

She looks up at him but does not reach for the vase of flowers. "The baby was a girl."

Frank turns away and clears a spot for the vase on a countertop close to the door. Then he comes to stand beside the bed, the profile side of Dusty that does not show the bruise and black eye. "Look, you know how you always say God has a purpose; sometimes we just don't know what it is."

"Stop it, Frank! Don't you dare go there! You," Dusty snarls at him, "have no right!"

Frank puts out his hands in a self-defensive gesture. "Calm down! Calm down. They'll come in here and sedate you if you get hysterical. Look, all I'm saying is maybe this happened for a reason. With your mother's help and my step-mom, they can babysit William, and you can go to college, just like you've always wanted. You know, to be like her." He gestured to me with a wave of his hand. "You'll have something to talk about other than dirty diapers."

"Go away, Frank. Get lost." Dusty smooths her blanket.

"Come on, honey, I'm kidding you. I want you to smile."

"I can't Frank; it hurts to smile."

The soft slap slap of Dean's loafers interrupts their conversation.

Frank looks over his shoulder and scowls at Dean. "Why don't you take Fran for a cup of coffee? Come back in twenty minutes, okay?"

The look Dusty gives Frank could melt an iceberg. "You don't give the orders here."

Dean folds his arms, leans ever so casually against the wall, and does not reply.

Frank shakes his head, as if we are an imposition, and then studiously ignores us, turning his back to Dean and me so that Dusty can only see him. "I have to work overtime tomorrow. Be there an hour early and leave an hour later. I'll come by after work. William is staying with your mother tonight and tomorrow. He's fine, really. Don't worry about us, okay?" He bends down close enough to kiss her, but Dusty blocks him with an up-raised hand.

"Go home. Go wherever. Just go."

Frank turns at the door before leaving with a parting shot. "You'll get over this, and everything will be fine. You'll see."

It is minutes before any sound comes out of her, the wracking sobs. Both Dean and I embrace her, none of us saying anything. Dean strokes her hair, and I hand her a box of tissues.

"Thank you, thank you, both. You sure you can do this for me? Help me leave? You're not afraid of Frank?"

"No," Dean snorted, "it's three against one. It always has been, always will be the three of us."

Dean can say something like that, and it sounds like the right thing to say, the right thing to believe.

"We are going to see Annie. If you need us, we'll be in the building, and you can text either one of us." Dean tugs the blanket and tucks it around Dusty's legs. "Try to get some rest. Okay?"

Dusty nods. I lean over and kiss her on the forehead. "I'll be here early tomorrow. We'll have a game plan, and you'll be all right. You *will* be all right."

"Okay." She blows her nose and nods vigorously. "Yes, I will be all right."

Dean and I leave her knowing that tomorrow we will engineer Dusty's escape from an abusive marriage and set the world right again.

As we're leaving, an older, matronly woman dressed in a grey pantsuit, white shirt, and sensible black walking shoes, clipboard hugged to her chest, bustles into Dusty's room.

Dean lifts an eyebrow and says in a low voice, "Social worker."

As we walk side by side down the busy hospital corridor to Annie's room, Dean and I do not speak to each other. Just before entering, Dean pauses and turns to me. "Let's go to my place from here where we can talk this thing out. I'm all by myself for the next week, so I'm thinking Dusty and William can stay with me." He waves me into the room. "That's our first move tomorrow."

I smile to see Annie propped up by pillows in bed, in spite of all the tubes snaking on her arms and sensors on her chest and fingers, looking regal, holding court with her parents. The difference is palpable, the tension gone from Annie's whole body. For the first time since I've seen her here, I feel hopeful she can get well. Dean feels it too, as he visibly relaxes as he shakes hands with Annie's father.

We talk openly about the treatment center Annie will be going to as an outpatient. Dean states again that it is a good choice and Annie has an excellent chance of a complete recovery. On that note, we say our goodbyes and leave to go to the lobby.

"Look outside," I say to Dean as we near the parking pay-ment box in the lobby. It is still early afternoon, and the sky has gone back to severe blue and cloudless. "Typical Seattle June weather: sun, rain, sun. I hope it doesn't snow tonight."

Before Dean can say anything, I blurt out, "Do you think Annie's going to make it? She looks so emaciated. How did that happen? Didn't Jon, her parents, for the love of all that is sa-cred, see what was happening to her?"

"*We* didn't." He puts a flat palm out up to silence me. "I know, I know, we saw her only once in a while, but you know she moved to Spokane to go to Gonzaga. She didn't come home that often. Her mother told me Annie hadn't been home for four months. I imagine she hid out in her apartment and pretty much stayed away from people." He leans on the wall. "Her father was the one who went to the university, brought her back home, and committed her to the hospital."

This is who we are, as we were, sharing our concerns for our friends. "The irony of it is her father smacked her and her sister and her mother around. I didn't think he cared wheth-er Annie existed. I remember Dusty felt abandoned by her father after her parents' divorce and his remarriage to Sylvia. There is a pattern here—fathers who don't care enough about their daughters."

"Maybe it's more like fathers who don't know *how* to care for their daughters."

"I cannot even imagine my father hitting me; he hardly ever raised his voice. My mother either." I picture my parents sitting at the dinner table, chatting about their day's events over a glass of wine. "I guess I lead a pretty sheltered life."

I flash back to a day in ninth grade when Dean came to school with a blackened eye. "Did your Dad ever hit you?"

Dean shakes his head. "No, no. Never hit me. I had a few run-ins at school. Brian."

"Porker? Not surprised, I guess." I look away and then back to him. "And you made nice with him at Colin's funeral."

"He's not a bad guy, Fran. Really." Dean snatches the parking ticket from me and pays for both his and mine. It turns out we parked on the same floor, so it makes it easy to follow him to his house. It's a small, brick house in the University district on a crowded, narrow street, but luckily both cars fit in his driveway.

"Do you want something to drink?" Dean opens the refrigerator door and points to an array of cartons of orange juice, apple juice, and a variety of cranberry blends. "Wine, too." He jerks his thumb to indicate a well-stocked wine cabinet.

"Water will be fine, thanks."

He swooshes the door shut. "Cheap date."

I look at him hard as he hands me a bottle of water. He is so prissy, I think.

Dean pours himself a glass of orange juice. "All right, step around the elephant, and let's talk about it in the living room."

There is always that moment when silence, like a rubber band, stretches through the memories and emotions. At first, there is so much to say, so much to convey, that it seems too much to even begin. Then the rubber band snaps.

Dean begins by handing me a pillow from the couch he sits upon, the end closest to the chair I chose. I take the pillow and wiggle and adjust until I feel comfortable.

"Fran—"

"You know my problems seem so petty," I say cutting him off, "compared to what Annie and Dusty are going through. You, you're such a good friend and always there to help. I know you and Dusty have been friends forever, and I don't want to taint that friendship. Dusty and I have put this argument behind us. We're good; we're friends again. We had a blowout, but now that seems so insignificant. I just didn't know."

"Your emotions are just as valid as anyone else's. You couldn't know how bad things were because Dusty didn't tell anyone. Not even me."

Dean can sound so doctor-ish, so patent sometimes. I notice he no longer stutters.

"But Fran, us. I never meant to hurt you. I really did not mean—"

"No, no, I'm sure you didn't mean to hurt me. You did though, you did, and so cowardly. Like I'm there at Dusty's wedding thinking one thing, and you both knew it wasn't ever going to be that."

"Cowardly? How did you get there?" The glass in his hand hovers near his lips.

"Oh, I'm in a crowd of people and so happy. If I had known otherwise, what you truly meant, do you think I would have been so *bubbly*? Not before the wedding because that might have spoiled the occasion, but to give me that necklace at the wedding and then spring on me you're gay as you did was cruel. Just plain cruel. And that look between you and Dusty—I saw her look at you quizzically. And why might I feel like a fool?"

Dean puts down his glass without sipping any juice. "You're right. You are so right. I didn't think that through." He wipes his brow with his hand. "By the way, Dusty and I were going to come down to Reed during the Renn Fayre. We had it planned and everything until she broke her wrist ice skating."

"Frank broke it during a fight. She threw a dirty diaper at him when he came home from spending the night with one of his girlfriends. Did you know on their wedding day, he was in the changing room with the girlfriend of his best man?"

No, by the look on his face, he did not know. Sometimes it feels good to have the last piece of the puzzle that makes the picture complete. But it hits me that Dusty really wanted to come to Reed for the weekend, and probably her planning to come with

Dean precipitated the fight with Frank. For all the control and violence, Frank still cannot completely dominate Dusty; it costs her big time with each rebellion, but the spark, that inner force of being so strong and creative, is still there inside her.

There may not be an elephant sitting in the middle of the room, but there is a tiger, hungry enough to eat us both.

Dean twists a ring on his left ring finger. A wedding band.

"You're married?" I sip from my bottle of water, relishing the coolness of liquid down my throat.

"Not formally. But we will be." He leans closer to me. "Fran, I think you'll like Marcus."

I doubt it, I think to myself.

He raises his glass in a toast. "To Referendum 74! To equality!"

"Yeah." I put my bottle back onto a coaster. "There's so little of it."

He drinks some juice and then deliberately works his glass onto a coaster, obviously buying some time; it's an old habit of his. "So, Fran, what about us? Can we be friends?"

I lean into the back of the chair and eye him steadily. I could never really hate him, and now I feel a hint of desire to be with him. But I will not let him walk this one out the door. "What you are really asking me is if I can trust you. No, not yet. Maybe with time we'll have something, another level of friendship. But it will never be the same." A bone to the tiger.

He shows his impervious little smile. "Never say never. It could be better than imagined." He throws a sirloin steak.

"Oh, shoot, I have so little imagination. Just ask my profs."

"Tell me about Reed. I want to know everything about your courses and professors and friends. Tell me all about that fantastic play you wrote and directed, *Angry Chickens*." He salutes me with his glass of juice. "I hear it is still quite the sensation on 'off-Reedway'—playing at the town hall, is it?"

I say, he says; we get caught up on our year we did not talk to one another. We share memories, mending our ripped friendship back together like pieces of fabric that make a patchwork quilt.

As if painting the scene, Dean brushes his hand in the air. "Do you remember the Washington State Fair?"

"Oh, yes, the last time we went. When Frank wouldn't let Dusty go on the rides with us."

"Yes, I thought it was so odd with you waiting in the car for us while she ran back upstairs to put on those stupid dangling earrings Frank had given her. We were going on the Hammer and Twirl-a-Whirl and the swings, for heaven's sake! And she wouldn't pull her hair into a ponytail because," I mimic how Dusty would say, "Frank doesn't like that."

"Remember when Annie got busted for shoplifting? How she changed from bad girl to saint?"

"Remember how we would line up our lawn jobs so we could go by Annie's house when she was on restriction and wave to her?"

"That was the year Colin died when the punk hit him with his skateboard. The same day you and Dusty gave that awesome presentation at the UW."

"And you tried to save Colin's life with CPR."

"That was the year we were the musketeers!"

"Let's see. You," I tap the air with my pointing finger at him, "were Athos, man of seemingly no romance in his soul; Dusty, Aramis, the religious one; Annie, D'Artagnan, the rash one." I lean over closer to him, "Remember how Annie could pronounce 'dar-TAN-yun' so beautifully with a French accent?" I sit straight back and place my finger delicately over my neck dimple. "I, the clothes-conscious Porthos. There is some irony in all that, you know."

"Oh, Fran of the understatement."

We laugh and we talk late into the evening, and bit by bit, a tenuous bond begins to form. The tiger pads out the room with the elephant close behind.

Dean walks me to my car, holding the door open until I have buckled my seat belt, and then leans into the opened window. "Tomorrow, then agreed, you come here by nine?" He raps the door with his knuckles. "Armor up, Musketeer."

"Yes, we'll spring the prisoner, whisk the princess and prince away from the Evil One." I turn over the engine and back down the driveway, confident with our working plan.

But you cannot rescue someone who isn't there.

Chapter 5

There are years that ask questions

and years that answer.

— Zora Neale Hurston

Dusty just disappeared. She and William are gone. On the third day of her disappearance, Frank filed a missing person's report. Dean, Dusty's mother, Dusty's father and his wife, Sylvia, Frank, and I are standing in a loose circle at the front desk of the downtown Seattle Police Department.

Hulking Frank stabs his finger inches from my face. "You! You were with her! You know where she is! Tell me where she is!" In all his ragged rage, he looks truly bereft. But I still think he is capable of murder.

"Well, that's not true," the officer, athletic and authoritative, says. Flipping through pages on his clipboard, he looks straight at Frank. "She checked out at 11:10 p.m., June 19, from the hospital after signing an order of protection."

"I was the last one to see Elizabeth." Mrs. Connor speaks softly, as though the effort of saying those words cost her an ounce of depleted strength. "She came by taxi. She said she would spend the night, but when I got up the next morning, she and William were not anywhere in the house. I thought maybe she had gone to a motel. She said she would never go back to Frank again. Never. Elizabeth said, 'The marriage is over.'" Mrs. Connor chokes back her tears.

After an awkward moment of silence while Mrs. Connor composes herself, the police officer says, "We can assume she left of her own volition, but we will make inquiries. I will need statements from all of you." The officer indicates a waiting area with benches. "Mr. Freeman, please follow me."

"You," he sneers at me as he passes, "you know where she is."

"I don't." Leaning into Dean's shoulder, I close my eyes and reassert, "I don't know where she is."

Mr. Connor paces, back and forth from one end of the bench to the other. Dusty's mother sits still, staring vacantly at her hands clasped in her lap. Dean snugs me closer to him, resting his chin on top of my head. The only one who is calm and cool is Sylvia, as if she has no interest in what is going on. How did I ever even think she was a caring person?

After twenty-five minutes, Frank barrels out of the interview room, glowering but wordless as he thrusts the door open and departs. Our little group, silent up to now, sighs collectively.

Dean and I are the last ones to be interviewed. It is an hour before I sit down with Officer Tanning and a fifteen minute interview. Dean, after I exit, slips in through the doorway and takes a seat. I stare numbly out the window as clouds scuttle by, much like the thoughts inside my head. I look around when Dean approaches, surprised that everyone else has left.

"Just you and me, kiddo." He extends his hand to pull me to my feet. "Let's get something to eat before I take you home. I have evening rounds."

Before Dean buckles his seat belt, I exclaim, "I know you said people can change. I just don't think they can. I can't imagine Frank changing."

Dean heaves a big sigh. "Frank wasn't always an angry guy. You know he had to give up his dream of being a professional baseball player when Dusty got pregnant. I wish she had been smarter and on birth control."

"As Dusty said, it takes two to make a baby. And *Frank* could have been smarter." Annoyed, I twist the hem of my t-shirt. "And his affairs? Can you justify that? I wonder if he ever gave a thought of getting and giving an STD. Poor, angry Frank, acting out his disappointments. Big man on the playing field, little man in life."

Buildings blur as we drive. We go to a nearby pizza parlor.

Seated in the nearly empty restaurant at three thirty in the afternoon, Dean looks intently at me. "How are you doing, Fran?"

I wave my hand, as if I could express myself with one grand gesture. "Funny how you can do something so normal, so casual, like ordering a pizza and Coke, after . . . after . . ."

"A gut-wrenching experience," he states flatly. "We do have more than our fair share of drama, don't we?"

"And you always say I am the queen of understatement." I chew my lip before going on. "Didn't you think Sylvia was a whole lot of casual? As if she was totally bored with the whole proceedings. I thought she cared—she gave me fifteen hundred dollars to give to Dusty! What is she all about? I feel like throwing the money back in her face."

Dean grows thoughtful. "I wouldn't be too harsh, Fran. I think there may be lot more to her than appearances."

With elbows on the table, I put my chin in my hands and say with mock sweetness, "I wonder, Dean, if I said black is the new color, would you say lilac, magenta?" I sip from my glass, purposefully loudly, and then look him in the eyes. "You always do that, counter what I say."

Just then the half-pepperoni, half-pineapple, Canadian bacon pizza plops down in front of us.

"Ahh," Dean scoops a slice of gooey, cheesy, pepperoni, "food for thought."

"Oww, the pineapple is hot!" I hurriedly sip my soda. "Maybe a message from God."

"Or just a reminder that you might have to eat your words."

To spite him, I take two bites and chew loudly.

He waggles his eyebrows, always a gesture that indicates he thinks he's won a point of argument. We eat in silence until I finish my last bite. I wipe the grease from my fingers and mash the napkin into the emptied pizza pan. "When," I lean across the table, "did you know you were gay?"

He blinks and then tosses his napkin onto the pie pan. "Well, it was not in a pizza joint." He stands, coming to my side. "Let's go to the park and talk for a while."

I think how ironic that the nicest thing about knowing another person for as long as I have known Dean is the comfort zone of our relationship that allows quiet space, not having to engage in useless chatter. On the drive to Gene Coulon Park by Lake Washington with a view of Mt. Rainier Park in Renton, we are both silent, and I absorb the quiet as a calming balm. Sun filters through the clouds, but my sweater feels just right as we walk along the water's edge.

Dean stops and points to a picnic table. "Let's sit. I want to talk about Dusty and Dean for a moment. I can't get out of my mind something. First, let me play the devil's advocate."

We would do this as an exercise all the time when we were in high school, especially for a term paper; one of us would take an opposing view or just try to find the most outrageous argument that the other would have to refute or support. I remember thinking in my freshman humanities class that game had taught me to weed out the insignificant ideas to get to the root of the idea and had impressed my professors that I could present a problem in layers.

"Let's look at what has happened from another perspective." I sit across from him, hugging my sweater close. "Dusty could not have gotten an order of protection in twenty minutes, nor could she have disappeared without a lot of organization. But there are underground organizations for battered spouses."

"What?" I bark. "Are you saying she had that already in motion when we were there?" I shake my head. "Pfft. I don't think so."

"No, I don't think she did. I think someone else did. I'm thinking her mother."

I sit up straight. "Remember that woman with the clipboard?"

Dean nods.

"Maybe she wasn't a social worker."

"Yeah, maybe not. The hospital staff, the police, and even Mrs. Connor were just too accepting of Dusty's disappearance. I know better than anyone that you maintain a professional demeanor, but all this time, it seems strange to me the lack of urgency. Except for Frank. And I really don't think he could kill her and William and then dispose of the bodies. He's not that cunning. And he has an alibi."

"You've overlooked his temper, what I think of as murderous rage." Although I have to grudgingly admit that I could not conjure a picture of Frank being that cold-blooded. Unless of course he killed in a spontaneous rage and then had to get rid of all the evidence. But then again, his alibi; he was at the Cowgirls bar downtown, left with a woman, and then closed the Admiral Pub. Apparently Frank went to her apartment after the bar closed, and he had witnesses at both bars and the woman's roommate. But he lied about working; he took three days' vacation from his job at Boeing.

"Now here's what I want you to think about. We have been so fixated on the monster Frankenstein; let's examine Frank the man."

"Oh, no, you are not going to excuse his behavior, are you?"

"Not at all. But, Fran, he is a person, not a characterization. He's more complicated than that. And give some credit to Dusty for loving him. He has good qualities. Remember how he treated his brother, Billy? And he didn't always bully Dusty. Think about it without prejudice."

"Well, Dr. Frazier, you might give him CPR, but I'm not so sure I would." I am irritated by his line of reasoning until he snags me.

"Oh, yes, I'm pretty sure you would Fran. It comes down to a question of our humanity, our ethics. and I'm certain that you would do the right thing in any case because you're a moral person."

I look at him steadily, rooting for a rebuttal. I change the subject. "Do you really think Frank had the talent to be a professional baseball player?"

Several Canada geese are milling about the vast green expanse of lawn. A particularly large one spreads his wings and, flapping and honking, chases another goose around in a circle. Dean and I watch for a moment, both us chuckling.

"It's funny you should bring that up because I was thinking of that earlier. Well, this is what I was thinking, relating it to myself. All throughout grade school, junior high, and college, I was pretty much of a whiz-kid—prestigious awards, scholarships, you know the candy for being smart. When I got into med school, suddenly I'm not the only bright boy around. I had some serious competition. You know what happened?"

I smiled. "You got your first C?"

"Something like that. I really had to work hard for not only the grades but also the positions—sort of like doing interviews all the time. It was an eye-opener, too. I think it is too bad Frank never had an opportunity to find out if he is truly good enough to play in the big leagues with other big boys. If he had pursued his career and found out he couldn't cut it, he might not have resented settling down with a wife, son, and good job."

"So, he has a reason for using Dusty as a punching bag."

"It's a lot easier to blame someone else than admit your own shortcomings. He is, after all, human."

"And not a very nice one. Although," I reply sarcastically, "he did buy her a very expensive espresso maker after he broke her wrist. Such a kind-hearted guy—she didn't have to go out anymore in the big, bad world to get a latte. And," I pause dramatically, "he brought *four* dozen roses this time when he kicked her in the stomach. I guess a baby is worth a little less than a coffee maker. Such a guy!"

Dean leans back on his elbow atop the table. "Well, this could affect some changes in him. We're all capable of change."

"I just don't think in Frank's case that'll ever happen. He's a first-class bully, and he's used to always having his way by dint of his magnitude, his size, his *entitlement*."

"I guess that depends on how bitter he is. He'll have to change his behavior, or he'll die a lonely, embittered old man."

I wonder if Dean means that for me as well. Can he have guessed I have been praying in our time together now, with the intensity of each minute we spend together, that he will realize he isn't really gay but wants a relationship with me and we would live happily ever after together? I switch back to the spoken topic and ask, "Do you really think he might take responsibility for his behavior? He was insistent to the very last minute that we are to blame for Dusty leaving him. I never saw or heard one single thing that would make me believe he would man up and admit she left him because of the way he treated her."

"He's going to have lots of time to think about it. He'll go through the stages of grief, anger, and denial. He could get stuck in any one of those stages, or he could work through them and mature into a better man." Dean looks down into his hands. "I'm pretty sure Dusty is not going back to him. It must have been the most heart-wrenching decision for her to leave. Everyone and everything she's ever loved is here; her mother, her friends, her life."

"She didn't even leave a note for her mom. I think that's scary, that's why I'm afraid . . ."

Dean takes my cold hand and warms it by sandwiching it between his two. "What could she say? Think about it. What could she say?"

At that moment I look at Dean's left hand, at the wedding band, and know we aren't in a fairy tale, and real life stories do not always have happy endings. I press our hands to my cheek, hold them tight, and weep.

"Oh, Fran, Fran," he soothes. "I know it hasn't been easy for you. I wish I had a good story to tell you to make it sensible, to make you understand about me." He wipes my tears with both of our hands. "I cannot pinpoint a time and place when I knew I was gay. A situation, maybe. Marcus is my age, met him my senior year when we scouted the prospective colleges. We hit it off because we are very much alike—at least superficially. Both young, smart, not into sports, not quite fitting in any place or group. I guess at one time when I had been talking a lot about you, he just hit me with 'choose, buddy' and it put it all out there."

I flutter my hand. "I'm so flattered to have been the deciding factor!"

"Stop it, Fran. It was not that easy for me."

I get as close as I can to his face. "We did everything *but*. Do you think it's that easy for me?"

He gets closer. "What do you want me to do? I cannot hit an undo button; I cannot change what is, Fran. Some things are just the way they are and will be. What is it you want from me? I am not going to apologize for being who I am."

No. Yes. Emotions upside down, all around. I swallow hard and look away and then glance at my watch. "Time to go, Cinderfella."

Dean reaches for and gently holds my wrist. "I'd like you to meet Marcus. He'll be home Thursday. Please come by. Friday?"

The warmth of his hand, the salty smell of his breath, the closeness of him. I slide my hand from his. "I don't know. I'll call you."

It is chit-chat on the way home. Both us, I think, realize we are at a crossroads with all the signs awry, leaving us direction-less. Nothing is quite resolved, and to make it all the worse, I still want him, still want him to be my lover.

Chapter 6

"It's been pretty hectic for you, hasn't it Fran?" My mom hands me a cup of coffee and sits beside me at the kitchen island. "How is Annie?"

"She's going to be released tomorrow. She'll go into a treatment program. It's going to take time, they say, for her to be well enough to be on her own. It's like a self-imposed prison."

"I think the key to understanding her anorexia is that it is a disease. She doesn't have control of the disease. Not yet. But I understand her mother and father are being very supportive."

I look over the rim of my cup. "Yeah, isn't that a twist of a family plot?"

"What about her sister, Elizabeth, or Betty? Is she close to Annie?"

"Bette, as she calls herself nowadays," I put my cup down, "isn't close to anyone. I think she moved to Nevada after she dropped out of college. Exotic dancer in Vegas is the rumor."

"Ah, what a waste of beauty and brains."

"Or," I punctuate the air with a finger, "she's living out her fantasy."

"As I said, what a waste."

"Oh, but really? What if she is *the* best exotic dancer of the West? Wouldn't that be fulfilling one's destiny? Who's to say that being a biologist, engineer, or doctor is better than being the person you have to be?"

"Well, I hope you are not trying to tell me that you have decided on a career as a circus performer."

I laugh out loud remembering the scene with Dusty in my bedroom when I put on the jester's hat. "I'm afraid I'd not be very good at it. Maybe a clown with big painted tears and a bulbous nose. Mute."

"Oh, that would never happen, Fran! You, not saying a word?" She leans back and laughs.

"I got you to laugh." I clink my cup to hers, and we drink our coffee.

"How's Grandma doing?"

My mother fidgets in her seat and then stills. "She's sleeping a lot lately. And slipping," she points to her temple, "confusing the past and present. People, places, time."

"The continuum shift."

"It's all very real to her."

I put my hand on her shoulder. "That's the beauty of it, Mom. It is real to her."

"It's not so real for the rest of us."

Our lively, depressing conversation is interrupted by the burping of the telephone. We must be the few anywhere that still have to have a landline because our cells drop calls. "I'll get it."

I expect a salesperson but instead recognize Scott's voice. "Fran? Hi!"

There is always that awkward moment of panic of what to say next, and inevitably, as now, I say something lame. "Hi, Scott. How are you?"

"Uh, um fine. I couldn't find your phone number, um, your cell. I took a chance that this would be your home phone. Hey! I was right!"

Well, his convo was lamer. At least, I reasoned, he's as nervous as I am, which surprises me as he always comes off as overly confident when I'm around him at Reed. "So what's new with you? Have you boxed any good books lately?"

"Oh, no. I've been working with my dad. He's got a big construction project in Kent, and I'm on the clean-up crew. You might say I'm the supervisor of the clean-up crew."

"Is it just a one-man crew?"

His laugh is deep and long. "Yeah, how'd you know?"

"Psychic. One of my many talents." Or basic psychology.

"Listen, Fran," he pauses, and I want to but do not interject that I *am* listening. "Would you like to go see the Impressionist exhibit at the Seattle Art Museum Friday? I could pick you up at eleven, and we could have lunch at the café at the museum after we see the exhibit."

I stifle a quick retort—or dinner—as I could spend a lifetime with Monet, Manet, Renoir, and especially Degas and Cézanne. "That sounds really nice. The house with the ginormous pink rhododendron by the parking strip."

"It's a date! See you Friday at eleven, Fran."

My mother arches an eyebrow. "Someone new? I could tell by your expressions."

I shrug, being used to my mother's acute observations. "Scott Nicholson. Seattle Art Museum. The Impressionists." I replace the phone in its cradle and stand there looking at it as if it might jump back into my hand.

My mom swivels and stands, tapping me on my shoulder. "I suggest you leave the clown outfit for another time."

My father has come into the kitchen, and I see the wink intended for my mother. "What's this? A young man come a-courting?"

"Yes, Dad. Scott Nicholson—he works for his dad in construction."

"Nicholson and Garry. Big outfit from the Eastside. Gainfully employed." He nods and smiles. "I approve."

I eyeball him and then my mother. "Sometimes I feel as if I'm still in high school."

Dad gets serious. "I was kidding you, Fancy Fran."

"I know, Popsicle, I know." I leave them to themselves, taking my cell phone outside. While I dial Dean's number, I notice Grandma has dug another hole beneath the rose bush. Maybe she's finding a way to China. She's spoken often of traveling in her retirement years.

It's a relief to get Dean's voicemail, and I leave a short three-sentence message. "Hi, Dean. Sorry something has come up for Friday. I'll catch you later."

Later he texts me, asking for another date and time. I don't reply.

I almost have myself convinced that I will answer his texts, return his calls, but I don't find the time. When he leaves to move back to Boston to do his internship, I do text him, wishing him all the best.

Horror vacui, nature hates a vacuum. I spend every day of my remaining vacation with Scott after he gets off work. We do activities together—hiking, canoeing, long walks around downtown Seattle, ferry rides, and an almost disastrous bike ride along the Burke-Gilman Trail. I like him a lot, and throughout the following school term at Reed, several people remark that we make a good-looking couple, a perfect twosome, someone said. No, I think at the time, just good enough. But I can't figure out what it is or isn't about the relationship that keeps me from feeling connected the way I felt with Dean.

Several of our friends are getting married the next summer, and we attend weddings and receptions as the next ones. Only I purposefully avoid catching the bridal bouquet every time it comes whizzing right for me. I don't spend as much time with Scott, as Annie has gotten out of the eating disorder program and is at home, piecing her life back together one day at a time. She is preparing for her wedding to Jon. It is not as painful to be around her now that she has gained forty pounds and looks normal again.

"Annie, you seem distracted and worried. Is there something bothering you?" I reach over and take her hand. "You know you can talk to me."

"It's all these details! I don't think it's worth it!" She pushes aside the brochures for wedding venues, limos, caterers. "It's all too much!"

"Annie, come clean with me. We've been friends too long, through too much. I know you. What is it?"

Tears stream down her face. She extracts her hand from mine and burrows her face into her hands. Her words, muffled and staccato, wrench my heart. "I can't have children. Ever." She sobs. "What's the point of getting married?"

"Does Jon know?" I frantically search my thoughts for something to say that will make a difference to this unexpected outburst.

She nods her head vigorously.

"Then if he's all right with it, isn't that the best reason to marry a man who loves you and whom you love? You love him, don't you?"

She nods even harder, mumbling, "Yes, yes, yes! But—"

"Well, that intrusive 'but' in my face."

She snorts a laugh, wiping tears from her face. "He's a good Catholic boy and said from the get-go he wanted a family."

"So adopt. Any problems with that?"

"Guys, ya know, want their own progeny. I don't want to wake up one day to see him full of regrets."

"Well, now there's an image I can't quite figure out."

"You know what I mean."

"Geez, Annie, there are options. Surrogate mother for one. And really how much do you know about the future? Anything, everything can change with new technology. We're in the renaissance, age of enlightenment with technology. You cannot give up hope for your future. You are here, alive, today. You of so little faith."

She examines me with a critical eye. "Yes, faith, that elusive thing with wings that flutters around my consciousness. I have asked myself, my broken self, how do I have faith when I am living in a fractured world?"

"You know what my dad said to me the day of Colin's funeral? He had no answers to the whys and wherefores either, but he has faith, and he said, 'I can be faithful, act as if I am full of faith.' I took it to mean that even in moments of despair, there is hope. We don't know if there is a tomorrow because we are conscious only today. There is no forever, only the moment we live in, but don't we, all of mankind, want to believe there is forever? That's why we marry and have children."

"Gads, Fran, I don't know if what you said is a commemoration or condemnation of marriage."

"Yes."

I smile and she smiles, throwing herself at me for a long and welcome hug.

I pull back and look at her critically. "Annie, there's something else bothering you. What is it?"

"Oh, Fran, it's this whole secrecy about my condition. I feel ashamed to have this eating disorder. I'm not supposed to talk about it—just to you and my therapist. Otherwise, I'm not really sick, I'm," she lowers her voice and shifts her eyes, "recovering. We don't mention the hospital, rehab, or treatment. You know, as if it's a secret not to be spoken out loud; no one is to know that I am all pieces glued back together."

I grab her by the shoulders and square off face to face. "Annie, you have a voice. Use it. Speak up, speak out about this disease and help others understand. You're good at helping others—you always have been—so use your experience to help others. Use *your voice,* so others can hear they are not alone. Don't hide behind secrecy—it'll only make you ashamed and miserable. And you are not that, Annie; you are not a miserable, scared little girl. You are a woman with a strong, beautiful voice and something to say. Say it. Leonard Cohen has a line in 'Anthem': 'There is a crack in everything / That's how the light gets in.' You're not broken, Annie, you're cracked a little like all of us."

She looks at me with her mouth agape. She nods, gulps, and says in a hoarse whisper, "I applied for admission to the UW. I want to go into social services." She scoops brochures through her hands. "You said it; you said what I have been trying to articulate. Thank you."

I reach over and toss a handful of brochures in the air. "Let's get these wedding plans organized, girlfriend! Before the day is here!"

We spend the whole day until suppertime making plans. Jon comes over after work, looking every inch the technical nerd he is with basic black-rimmed glasses, shaggy hair in need of a cut—no, in need of a style, khaki pants with bulging pockets stuffed with note papers, and offers to take us both to dinner. I decline, as it is my turn to make dinner for my parents and me.

I crawl through cross-town traffic; it takes me an hour to get home.

Mom and Dad are sitting at the dining table; two glasses of wine have been poured but not imbibed. Dad has his hands wrapped around my mother's hands, and I can see she is shaky.

Dad looks up, meeting my eyes. "Join us, Fran. We have some bad news."

You ever just want to bolt? Run away to some exotic locale with palm trees swaying in the tropical breeze, ukuleles strumming in the background while you loll on the beach without a care in the world? With my luck there would be a rogue wave that would wash me out to sea.

I pull a chair to sit next to my mother. My mother, the strong invincible one, the one who catches a crisis like a professional baseball player and manages the play. She, who rarely cries, is crying now.

"Dad, is it Grandma?"

Mom nods and Dad sighs. "Yes," he says. "She fell and broke her hip. She's out of surgery and, after rehab and therapy, will have to go into an assisted living home."

"She just kept begging me to take her home, and I had to keep repeating 'I can't, I can't.'"

I have never seen my mother sob like this. I reach over to her and rub her back. I have nothing to say.

"We cannot leave now," she sputters, and I don't understand what she means. "I just couldn't leave her," my mother adds.

Ding! The bell goes off inside my head. My parents' thirtieth wedding anniversary is in two weeks—they are going on a cruise to Alaska with a week's stay in Victoria, Canada. "Mom, listen to me. You have to go. I'll be here, and I'll go see

Grandma every day; that's a promise. Uncle Ryan is here. We've got you covered."

"No," she shakes her head vehemently, "she's my mother."

"And my grandmother. We're all family, remember?" I immediately feel that I have spoken too abruptly, like thumping her upside the head. "Let me do this for you, Mom. Please. In two weeks, Grandma will be where she's going to be in the home that I'm sure you have researched to find the best one, getting good care. I'll make sure she gets good care. What sense does it make for you not to go? I'm here, and I'll take care of the house and Grandma. Don't cancel your trip. Have some faith in me that I can do this."

She blinks several times, trying, I suppose, to put me in focus.

I wave a tissue at her. "Here, your nose is running."

She disengages her hands from my dad's hands and takes the tissue. Laughter bubbles up from her, then Dad, then me, all of us getting the humor in the switch in the parental role.

My dad sniffs the air. "What did you put in the crock pot that smells double delicious?"

"*Boeuf bourguignon.* Sorry about the butchered pronunciation. Annie has tried to teach me the correct way to say these things, but I have not the knack of the nasal."

"Well, I'm impressed!" Dad places his hand over his stomach.

"Don't be; it's a simple recipe," I say as I get up and move to the kitchen. I put the dishes out and then get the flatware. "You know me; simplicity is my motto."

"I'll do clean-up as my part," Dad volunteers. "Are you going out with Scott later?"

I serve, and it is gratifying to see them both relish the first mouthful because the beef stew did turn out delectable. "No, he has plans with friends. He's twenty-one, you know. Party time."

I lean close to my mother. "I'm always the designated driver, and I don't particularly enjoy all those repetitive, stupefying jokes or his friends. It's better he has his play dates with friends and I have mine."

Dad sets his mouth in that way of his that means a word or two of wisdom will be forthcoming. "Most young men go through this phase. Have patience; it'll pass."

"You know me, Dad, patience personified."

Dinner is done, and I push back my chair to grab plates to take to the sink. My dad goes in the kitchen with his hands full of dishes. I follow, surprised to hear my cell chime for an incoming text. I put everything on the counter and pick up my phone. I am mildly surprised the text is from Dean: "Home for the duration." Whatever that means. No matter, he's home. It's now, and I've got some mending to do. I get cold chills and realize that I had better do something quickly, or I might lose another friend I love. "Excuse me; I need to answer this."

I go out on the waterside deck. It will be a beautiful sunset tonight with promises of reds and pinks streaking the clouds over the Olympic Peninsula. When my world shifts on its axis and people fall off, the physical world keeps going on from sunrise to sunset. I need to right my world, so that I am not the only one in it.

"Yes," I type, "I would like to meet Marcus. Tonight, 8."

I go to my room and take the box with the necklace out of the drawer and sit with my phone on the edge of my bed to Google the meaning of the stones. I touch each stone as I read about it. Ruby, given as a gift, symbolizes friendship and love. Sapphire is peace, happiness, communication, intuition, and insight. Blue topaz is courage and overcoming fears; it is the stone for writers, scholars, artists, and intellectuals. Emerald promotes self-knowledge and peaceful dreams and encourages balance and patience. Citrine is said to open the mind to new thoughts and balance in one's life.

And the bail, the fleur-de-lis, the national flower of France. I rub it gently between my fingers. A symbol for the musketeers: Dean, Fran, Dusty, and Annie.

Obviously, Dean designed this with thoughtful intent. That is one of the many things I love about him, how much thought goes into what he intends. The little heart's diamond twinkles in the inscription, "4ever & a Day."

I shove the box with the necklace into my purse. The necklace that Dean gave me. The one with the broken chain.

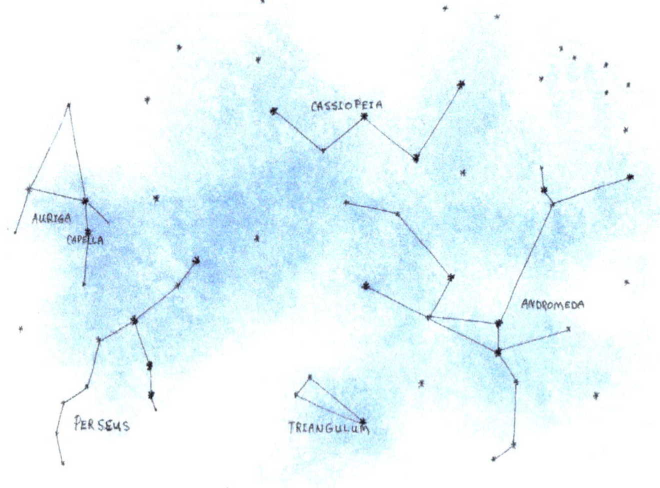

CASSIOPEIA
AURIGA
CAPELLA
ANDROMEDA
PERSEUS
TRIANGULUM

Chapter 7

Dean sweeps his hand in a grand gesture to welcome me as the door widens for my entrance. The first impression one gets upon entering the room is that every item in the room has its place. Not exactly over-orderly but with careful consideration for balance, texture, and color. It must be Marcus's doing because Dean is generally indifferent to his immediate environment. I would always be wary of tripping over his running shoes.

"Fran, I would like to introduce you to Marcus."

He startles me by materializing beside Dean. Taller than Dean in crisply ironed shirt and denim jeans, darker hair, and no-rim glasses, Marcus has even features short of handsome, green eyes framed in thick eyebrows, a soul patch on his chin.

"So glad to meet you!" I offer my hand for him to shake. "You must be the wizard of the home. I don't remember this place being so well-tended." I fluster. "I didn't mean that as a back-handed compliment. Really, your place is beautiful."

"Thank you, m'lady. I rather like being thought of as wizard. It took some magic to tidy this up when," he jerked his thumb, indicating Dean, "the master of clutter lived alone."

"All right, now that you two have hit it off using me as a Ping-Pong ball, shall we make ourselves comfortable in the living room?"

"And not the rec room?" I follow Marcus as Dean comes to my side.

"Thank you for coming. It means a lot to me."

"The night's not over. Marcus might not like *me*."

But the night speeds through the hours with small talk and catching up and knowing each other's histories. Dean has decided on pediatrics, and Marcus already has a job as an environmental engineer with the Office of Sustainability and Environment.

"So, Fran, what's after Reed?" Dean gulps the last of his green tea.

"I'm graduating ahead of schedule and doing my graduate studies at the UW, starting in October." I put down my teacup, waving away the proffered refill. "No, thanks. No more tea for me, Marcus."

"We're all going to be Huskies! Woof!" Marcus puts the teapot back in the exact spot it came from on the tea tray and then the tea cozy over the teapot. "We'll wear our Husky shirts under our wedding finery."

"When's the wedding?"

Dean has color in his cheeks and a grin I remember so well. "Next March."

"You know Annie's getting married in January? I've spent hours, and I mean that literally, with the wedding plans. I will not be a bridesmaid ever again."

"How about my best person at my wedding?"

Marcus picks up the tray. "If you will excuse me, I'll just get these out of the way."

As he leaves, I take the box with the flowers and dove necklace from my purse.

Dean sits back, stunned. "You're giving it back to me? You came over tonight to give this back to me?" He tucks his hands beneath his legs, refusing to take the box I offer to him.

"Yes, on one condition. You have the chain fixed and give this back to me on my birthday. I am not going to wear a Husky shirt underneath a formal, but I will want to wear my necklace."

He hovers for a moment and then ever so gently, ever so Dean, he reaches for and takes the box. "Fran . . . of course I will."

"I said something to Annie today as she was having a meltdown that made me really stop and think about what's important to me. I know this might seem counter-intuitive, but I told her that there is no forever, only the moment we live in, but it made me think of how much you mean to me and I want to be with you forever. If not as a lover, then as your friend. Life is so fragile, so unpredictable with our loves and friends and family. I cannot *not* have you in my life. You mean too much to me."

"Then can we plan to be together on your birthday?"

I hadn't thought about how that would work, introducing Scott to Dean. "You, me, Marcus, and Scott. At least for an hour or so sometime during the day would work for me if that is good for you."

"Why not here? Let me know what's a good time, and we'll make it happen." He rises as I stand up to leave. "But we'll get together before then. Maybe the three of us could meet for a late lunch or early dinner between our schedules."

I detour to the kitchen where I catch Marcus's attention with a wave. "I'm glad we finally got to meet one another. It's been a terrific evening. Thanks."

He wipes his hands down his jeans, which surprises me; it seems an uncharacteristic thing for him to do. "M'lady," he takes my hand to his lips, "it's been a pleasure."

When Dean and I get to my car, I stop before getting in. "Have you ever heard from Dusty? I thought maybe if anyone would hear from her, it would be you."

"No," he shakes his head, his face a map of sadness, "not a word. I miss her, too. Sometimes I think I'll give her a call and tell her something. It hurts when the realization hits me she isn't here."

"Yes, it hurts." We stand silently sharing our moment of grief. "Look at the beautiful night sky with all those stars. Do you think there are sentient beings out there?"

"Yes, I do. I think they are too intelligent to visit this world."

"Maybe," I say, leaning into him, "this is the sandbox where we, like toddlers, learn how to share and learn social skills."

"Look, Fran." He points to the night sky at the constellations. "Lyra, Ursa Minor, Cassiopeia. There! Hercules, the fifth largest of today's constellations. It was Ptolemy in the second century that found and named it."

"Is there any subject you don't know?"

"One or two."

Then we hug, and I swear I feel a paradigm shift, that my world has righted itself.

I spend several more hours of the week, which I dub "Annie planning," with Annie. She and I also spend time with Dean and Marcus, and I spend time with Dean, and Dean and Marcus. In between, I visit my grandma in the hospital for mercifully brief visits as she drifts off frequently and for longer periods. Although, by the time she is transferred to the rehab center for therapy, she has more lucid minutes each day. My mother finally admits she feels comfortable going on her trip and leaving me with the responsibilities of tending the roses, yard, and Grandma. I tell her I will even fill in the holes that Grandma has dug.

During the evenings I have by myself, I think a lot about my relationships. I ask myself why I feel hesitant to introduce Scott to Dean, to Dean and Marcus. I realize that I have lopped off a whole section of my life from Scott's, keeping a lot of my past from him. Not that I am ashamed of it; I just do not want to share it. I want it all to myself. In effect, I am straddling between real commitment and dilettantism.

Scott and I never have had a fight—we simply discuss the issue and resolve it—until the subject of Dean and Marcus comes up over the phone late one night.

"But Scott, one night this week isn't too much to ask of your time. I want you to meet my friends, Dean and Marcus."

"Your gay friends? Really?"

"Dean and I have been friends since grade school, Scott. Gay or not, we're friends with a long history."

"Well, you know how you don't like hanging out with my friends? I don't want to hang out with your gay friends."

"Unlike certain friends of yours, Scott, my friends will treat you with respect. I can guarantee that."

"Geez, Fran, getting hit upon by a guy is a compliment for a woman. But a guy getting hit on by another guy is not what I consider complimentary."

"I seriously doubt that either Dean or Marcus would find you attractive. They are committed to each other. In fact, I will be standing up for Dean at their wedding." I try to relax the stranglehold I have on the phone.

"I don't think that's a good idea, Fran. I won't be there."

"Okay, I won't insist if it makes you uncomfortable. I wish you would reconsider—"

"Fran, did you not hear me? I don't like the idea you will be there. I don't want you to be there either!"

"So, we'll do a trade-off? Two of your objectionable friends for two of mine?" He'd better understand sarcasm.

"You know, it's different, okay? My friends are normal, red-blooded men. Not . . ."

"Not what, Scott?" I can imagine what the fill-in-the-blank word would be.

"You know something, Fran? This explains a lot about you. I think maybe you don't really like real men; you don't want to be in a man-woman relationship. Maybe you should give some thought to *your* sexual orientation."

I do not cut him off abruptly but whisper, "Goodbye," and hang up. Nor do I cry knowing it is over. I finally have the answer to why I did not want to make a commitment to Scott; underneath the facade of his college education, he was a good ole boy.

DAILY JOURNAL
PHOTOGRAPHS

Chapter 8

Truths and roses have thorns about them.

— Henry David Thoreau

I have the day to myself after dropping my parents off at Pier 91 to board the Alaskan cruise ship. My mother was unusually quiet during the morning preparations to leave, and I jabbered non-stop to fill the void. Grandma has recovered and is doing well enough to leave the rehab center. Just three days ago, a family group of us moved her into her room at the new home. It is a good-sized room with a big picture window overlooking the well-tended gardens; it was large enough for Grandma's small recliner situated close to the television, always on, and a metal folding chair. My mother hung Grandma's favorite seascape painting on the blank wall next to her bed, done by an artist she had met years ago, and brought her the blue-and-yellow patchwork quilt she had made for her, and Uncle Ryan peopled the dresser with photos of family, mostly him with his boys. Grandma reveled in the attention, just as she always did when Mom, Uncle Ryan, his two sons, spouses, and I had surrounded her while she held court. The heartbreak for all us, especially my mother, was when Grandma announced it was time to go home—whose car would she be riding in? Five of us quietly bled out of the room, leaving Mom and Uncle Ryan with Grandma. Uncle Ryan, in his brusque way, tried to make her understand she was home, which upset Grandma so much she latched onto my mother's hand and pleaded to go home with her. After what seemed hours, probably in reality fifteen minutes, Mom and Uncle Ryan joined our motley crew in the lobby. After all the histrionics, Grandma drifted, came back, and talked about how she always liked living there in the condo with such lovely landscaped grounds.

I am restless, and after rereading yet another page of *Magic for Beginners*, I turn off the Kindle. The one thing I can do for my mother is pack up Grandma's belongings in the empty boxes in her room. I'd call my Grandma a "neatnik," so well organized is her room, unlike mine. She has a journal with a fat, black pen on the nightstand next to her bed. I hesitate before I sit on the bed and open it. Pasted inside the front of the journal is a typed poem, "One Perfect Rose":

> A single flow'r he sent me, since we met.
> All tenderly his messenger he chose;
> Deep-hearted, pure, with scented dew still wet—
> One perfect rose.
> I knew the language of the floweret;
> "My fragile leaves," it said, "his heart enclose."
> Love long has taken for his amulet
> One perfect rose.
> Why is it no one ever sent me yet
> One perfect limousine, do you suppose?
> Ah no, it's always just my luck to get
> One perfect rose.

I laugh out loud, feeling at that moment a thousand connections to my grandma, for I had read that same passage and highlighted the page in my book of collected poems of Dorothy Parker. I flip through the pages, a twinge of guilt for snooping pinching me, but go ahead and read a few of her most recent entries.

All these voices whispers of ourselves that should be heard

memories are puzzle pieces, capturing moments in our lives to piece together as a puzzle

My mind, so clear some days like an endless blue sky. Then my thoughts, like wispy clouds, almost real memories floating. I can't quite capture . . . some days it rains from dark clouds. I am overwhelmed by sadness of what I cannot remember.

I put the journal down, my hand resting on the cover feeling the waves of melancholy wash over every part of me, imagining Grandma in a lucid moment writing this. I will take this with me when I go see her this afternoon, give it to her. Then I remember the photo album, and after looking in desk drawers, dresser drawers, underneath the bed, I find it in the closet on top of a locked metal document box. The box is about the size of a shoebox. Whatever object is in there makes a muffled noise when I shake the box.

Once again, I sit on the bare mattress to browse through the photographs, many of them of people and places unfamiliar to me. I recognize my mother in old black-and-white pictures that captured her maturing from a toddler to a young woman in a new Easter outfit. I really like the baby pictures of her, especially a series of a golden retriever running alongside her, naked with a discarded diaper behind her.

Of course, I am more interested in the picture Grandma showed me of the man named George. I pry behind each photo carefully with my fingernail until I find it. There is another one I find, one where my grandma is in a satiny formal dinner dress, beside George and another one with George and some other man. Upon looking closer, I think it might be my grandfather, Karl, as a young man, and the picture Grandma showed me of her as a young woman on a picnic with George. It occurs to me that someone else was there taking the picture.

And there is something else about the photograph of George that alerts me, but it is elusive. I look again, very closely. Something about his smile. I flip back to the pictures of my mother in her Easter outfits, and there is one of her smiling directly at the camera, a very similar pose to the one of George in his tuxedo.

I put the photos all back as I found them. Then with the journal and photo album together, I leave the room to get ready to go see Grandma.

She is awake, sitting up in bed sipping a cup of tea. "Fran! My goodness, if I'd known you were coming, I still wouldn't have baked a cake." She puts aside her cup. "Seems I can't do much of anything lately."

"Hi, Gram." I kiss her forehead with a loud smack. "How are you?" It's an auspicious sign that she knows who I am.

"I have been better, thank you anyway." She points to the walker. "I hate that damn thing. I'd rather use my cane, but I can't find it."

This isn't going to be easy with Grandma in one of her dark moods. "I'm thinking that when your hip is totally healed, you'll be able to use your cane again. And by the way, Gram, I brought you something." I put the journal down beside her with the pen clipped to the front cover. "I thought maybe you would like to write in it."

She stares at it for a long moment before she sighs, takes the pen, and lays it in her lap. She turns her hands over, tracing age spots with a finger on her left hand. "Look at my age spots. Maybe if I connected them with a magic marker, my whole life would come together as a puzzle does."

"Well, how about this? I also brought your photo album." I scoot my chair close her bedside. "I'd like to ask you some questions about the pictures you showed me."

I watch her intently as she thumbs through the album. She pauses. "This is your other grandmother. You called her Mimi. There's a story behind that."

"Actually that's great-grandmother, but—"

"You were just four and eavesdropping when I was pointing out to your father that all that woman does is talk about 'me, me, me'; after that you wouldn't call her anything but Mimi. And she thought you were so clever to have a special name for her!"

"I haven't heard that story before. Um, Grandma, who's taking the picture here, where you and George are sitting on a blanket?"

She smiles at me, kind of a goofy look that I know means she is drifting away.

I am desperate to hold onto the thread of truth that connects to her memory. "Grandma! Can you tell me who this is and who is taking the picture?"

She flicks her hand weakly, dismissing me. "I am an old woman now. I forget things." She closes her eyes, and I know I've lost her. As I start to get up, she says to someone, or no one, "Then it all comes back to me, and it is too much. I am tired, tired to my bones."

I leave the photo album within reach, take the pen, and clip it back onto the cover of the journal before I leave.

And it goes pretty much the same day after day. Some days she is happy to be there; some days she implores me to take her home. I bring her a bouquet of shades of red roses from her George Best rose bush, and she bursts into tears.

"Grandma! I didn't mean to make you cry!" I swipe at her tears.

She grabs my hands and brings them to her lips to kiss. "It's okay, pet. You've made me so happy."

She certainly doesn't look happy.

"Fran," she pulls me closer, and I dread that she might beg me to take her home with me. Why didn't I think this thing through? Of course roses from her beloved bush would trigger an emotional outburst. "Fran," she whispers, though there is no need, "if you won't take me home with you, do me a favor, please?"

I pull back a bit, my hands still lassoed by hers. "If I can I will."

"Beneath the rose bush, I buried a half-pint Mason jar. It has a key in it that will unlock the metal box on the upper shelf of my closet at your house. Bring those to me. Tomorrow."

"Grandma, all this time you were trying to unbury something?" Well, another upending of an assumption.

"Yes, yes, I'm older and just a bit wiser." She shakes our hands and lets go of mine. "I realize that I cannot bury my past." She examines her hands for several minutes. "These brown age spots on my hands . . . when I was young, they were freckles." She draws her finger along, connecting them with an imaginary line. "These are the stories of my life."

"I'll go right home and find that key. Grandma, I love you." I kiss her as she closes her eyes and decamps.

I spend three hours digging a five foot moat with a spade around the rose bush without finding anything but rocks. I throw the spade down, near tears. Maybe the jar fell down a rabbit hole and landed in Beijing. It takes an hour to fill the trough back in with dirt, and by that time all I want are a cold drink and a shower.

Exasperated with everything, even the steady plopping of droplets from my wet hair, I sit staring at Puget Sound. What am I going to tell Grandma? I've never broken a promise made to her.

The mind works in ways a lot like a computer, scrolling through the subconscious for answers in stored memory. Out front is a huge bubble-gum-pink rhododendron. When I get my laptop, I type in the browser what I know it is, Rhododendron Loderi, and up pops pictures of the Rhododendron 'Loderi King George.' If my hunch is right, I'll find that jar.

It only takes me forty minutes to find it with a shovel this time. And the bonus: the bush got some needed TLC.

I get to Grandma's room earlier than I have any day previously. She is flipping through the photo album too fast to really see anything but a blur, I am sure.

"Gram! I found the jar!" I hold it up for her to see that the seal has not been broken and the key is still encased in a wad of wrapping paper. "It was beneath the rhody."

She studiously ignores me. I sit down in the padded folding chair and wait for her attention.

"Gram . . ."

She throws the album at me, but it lands short of hitting me and skids to my feet. "I don't like it here. I want to go home!" She impales me with her stare.

It feels as if I am superglued to the chair; I can't move or speak, but every breath I take sounds in my ears like a steam engine laboring up a mountainside. It might have been a minute, it might have been an eternity when I realize someone is standing next to me.

The nurse lays her hand on my shoulder. "Your grandmother is having a bad day."

"Really." I nod.

Grandma hunches over and glares without replying.

The nurse approaches Grandma but stays out of harm's reach. "Mrs. Karlson, Dr. Smith will be in to see you in five minutes. I'm afraid I have to ask your granddaughter to leave."

Finally able to move, I gather the scattered pictures up, shove them into the album, get my wallet and the box, and leave.

I am still pretty shaken up when I get home, thrown into a whirlwind of self-recrimination, blaming myself for setting her off with the roses the day before, scared at the monster in her, and mad that it was this way. I was so curious to know what is in the box, so sure it has something to do with my history, and now all I want to do is pitch it in Puget Sound. I do not want to ever go back to the home and see Grandma. That woman is not the person who is my grandmother. She may have had her mean, petty, little ways, but she never, ever, would do bodily harm to me.

The phone rings, and I literally jump out of my chair. My hand is shaky when I answer.

Dr. Smith introduces himself and explains my grandmother's behavior. "And it is typical behavior of Alzheimer's patients. Please try not to take it personally. She'll have no recollection of this incident." He pauses.

Not take it personally? How else do you take an act of aggression? I sweep my hair from my forehead, trying to think clearly. "Did I make her mad? I brought her roses from her favorite bush, and I think I may have stirred up some bad memories." No, I mean *sad* memories.

"Miss Reed, I assure you, you did not make her mad. I repeat, this is typical behavior of the disease in advanced stages. Tomorrow she won't remember any of it."

"Oh! You think I should come back?" I don't think I want to do that. "Okay, yes, I'll come around the same time as the other days when she seems more like my grandmother. Thank you. Goodbye."

Advanced stage—I know what it means. You can bury your head in the Kindle for only so long before the reality of the situation becomes apparent. But a little voice inside my head reminds me that we are all in an advanced stage of life; the minute we are born, we move towards our death. Not that it is all that comforting to know my grandmother is never going to be the person I loved before, but I find solace in having had her throughout my life so far. And I will love her until the day she dies.

What to do with the box? And the key? "Curiosity compels me" is a refrain through my head. I think the right thing would be to wait for my mother and discuss it with her when she comes back from her trip. But isn't it funny how you can make a solid resolution and it turns out to be as substantial as a cloud?

It is Grandma who makes the decision for me. I skip a day before going back to see her, and I go no earlier, no later than I did on her good days.

She perks up with a radiant smile. "Hello, my favorite granddaughter!"

I'm her only granddaughter, but today this is the best salutation I've ever heard, and I feel a tingle of happiness throughout my whole body.

"Hugs and kisses!"

I hesitate only for a split second, but I am still ashamed that it was my first impulse.

She traces her finger along my cheek. "I've been thinking."

No irony in that.

"I want you to open that metal box. There is something I want you to have. You will find some papers. You must share those with your mother. And a ring. I want you to have the ring."

"Grandma, I could bring the box here, and you could open it."

"No, Fran, please don't. You'll understand it all better after you open the box. I used to think of it as my Pandora's box."

"Geez! Maybe I don't want to let out all those ills upon us!"

"Ah, but," she taps the air with her finger, "hope was left behind. And I *hope* empathy."

"Oh, Gram, you've never done anything to be forgiven for."

"And, young lady, how would you know? You're not your mother."

I ease away, backing off to the folding chair far enough from her that she can't reach me, and keep a lightness in the tone of my voice. "I am my mother's daughter and your granddaughter; that's how I can be certain of what I say."

She grunts. "You're young yet. You'll learn. You've got heartache in your future, that much I know."

I blow her a kiss from the doorway. "I know, Grandma, I know."

Chapter 9

Annie calls just as I come into the house. "Now?" Trying on bridesmaid dresses is not something I look forward to, even less so on a summer day in July. "Give me an hour. Oh, all right! Thirty minutes. I'll meet you there."

The box will have to wait to be opened later. The hours I spend with Annie at the wedding shop with one dress after another seem endless, as the wedding itself seems too far away.

"Fran! This one!" She has chosen a strapless magenta gown, quite elegant in its simplicity.

"I thought your theme was blue?" Though, the dress is very flattering on me, which is a pleasant surprise after the seven others she did not like.

"I think I've changed my mind. I can have the same color sash for my wedding dress. And the guys can have matching cummerbunds. Oh! this is going to be so perfect!"

"I hope it doesn't snow."

She gives me a withering look. "We'll be inside the church, Fran. With two hundred people, it'll be plenty warm enough."

My shorts half pulled up, I hop around to get in her face. "Annie! When did this become a celebrity event?"

"We have big families, Fran," she chirps, expanding her hands as she continues. "One over here, two over there, his side, my side, and mother, father, grandparents, cousins, friends. Get the picture?"

"Have you talked to your sister, Elizabeth? Will she be in the wedding?"

She collapses her hands. "No, she wishes me the best but will not come back here even for my wedding."

I pull my t-shirt over my head. "In a perfect world. But you know, she might change her mind. There's a lot of time for reconsideration."

Annie looks at me with a wry smile. "Fran, ever the optimist. Really, I just hope the groom shows up; I really don't care about anyone else."

I arch an eyebrow and shoot her a look. "I'll be there," I wave to the dress, "in my formal. And so will Dean, and so will Marcus. We'll go do karaoke."

She guffaws. "Not one of you can carry a tune. Yes, that would be a hoot!" She gets serious. "If Dusty were here, it'd be as if we were the musketeers again."

That hurt. "Yeah, I've thought the same. I think about her a lot. I hope, no, I pray she's all right. I wonder what part of the world is she in."

"What about Scott? You guys get past that glitch?"

"Let's go get something to eat, and I'll tell you about it."

We go to a Mexican restaurant across the street, and during the course of the meal, I fill her in on the last conversation I had with Scott, the same basics I already told her about but apparently she was not listening too closely.

Annie asks for a take-home box and scoops most of her meal into it. I push my nearly empty plate aside and point my fork at her. "Brides usually lose weight; you are going to have to do better if you want to wear that size ten."

"I *am*. I'm a size eight. I have to work at it, and it's not easy, I can tell you that. Not with all eyes on me every time I put my fork down."

I lower my fork. "Well, you did a good job on that, I guess. You are looking really healthy. Like your old self."

"Thank you, Mother Fran."

She stops outside the doors of the restaurant. "Fran, I'm sorry I haven't been much of a friend to you, especially lately. I didn't realize you and Scott had broken up, that it was really over. I guess I've been self-absorbed and not paying attention as I should."

It's an awkward moment, as I am always uncomfortable when someone apologizes to me. "Oh, Annie, you're my friend through thick and wedding." I give her a quick hug and a promise to see her at the end of the week.

I try not to think of Dusty, but flashbacks stream throughout my thoughts. I have a painting she did for me of Paris in 1625, peopled with historical figures from Dumas's *The Musketeers*: Louis XIII, Cardinal Richelieu, de Tréville, Milady. In it, Dean, Annie, Dusty, and I are the musketeers. The picture is framed and hung on my wall next to a photograph of Annie, Dusty, Dean, and me where I see them every day. So long ago it was when we were all for one and one for all. Now that's history.

I'm satiated and exhausted from my outing with Annie. Sitting on the deck with my Kindle, I fall asleep and wake with a start. I actually forgot about Grandma's box. It takes several times running hot water over the jar before the rusted lid budges and the pop resounds in the too-quiet house. Once unwrapped, the key is tarnished, and I rummage around the garage until I find some WD-40. Finally, the key slips in the lock.

I snatch the velvet ring box and wrench it open. And gasp. It is the most beautiful piece of jewelry I have seen. It is a thick gold band with an oval ruby surrounded by diamonds that continue down the sides; I cannot read all the inscription inside, but part of it, "to my lov." It does not quite slide onto my right ring finger. I stare and stare at it, turning it this way and that; it is such a beautiful ring.

When I unroll the leather document keeper, the first piece of official paper is my mother's birth certificate. Only this isn't right. It reads "Teresa Georgette Bernard"; my mother's maiden name is Karlson, Teresa Lynette Karlson, just like on her high school diploma, her BA in fine arts, and her master of fine arts. The next official paper is a divorce decree, stapled to a marriage license, my grandmother and George Samuel Bernard; the next one is a marriage certificate of my grandmother to Isaac Karlson; and the last one, a copy of adoption papers by Isaac Karlson with my mother's correct birthdate and name change. And a photo is beneath all the papers.

In the photo, my grandmother is holding a baby girl, my mother; beside her is George, so handsome in a suit and tie. But it is an odd picture. He is looking fiercely at the camera, unsmiling, with his hand not quite on my grandmother's shoulder, as if he is leaning towards the camera and pushing away from her and the laughing infant with her eyes focused on him, as are my grandmother's eyes. She is half-smiling, as if she had asked him a hopeful question. It is a disturbing picture, and inscribed on the back is "June 23, 1951, the last kiss." The divorce was finalized February 15, 1952, and the marriage to Isaac Karlson, May 21, 1952.

I don't know how you can be stunned breathless yet not all that surprised, but I am because so many little puzzle pieces fit together to make this picture. Two scenarios occur to me: my grandmother had an affair with Isaac and George found out, or George left my grandmother and his daughter for someone else.

My mother and I wear the same ring size, so I figure if I have it resized, she can wear it until she gives it to me. I argue with myself all the way to the jeweler's that the ring really isn't mine, even if Grandma said I could have it; the ring really belonged to my mother. Oh, but I want to wear it and have it for mine.

Two days later, the jeweler calls to say it is ready. I agonize how to approach the subject with my mother, and today is the day to pick my parents up at Pier 91 at four thirty. When Mr. Black slid the ring onto my finger, we both just looked at it a minute. He gently turned my hand to show the sparkling ruby and diamonds. "The ruby is the precious stone that is symbolic of passionate commitment, love, and powerful feelings. From very ancient times, it was considered the perfect wedding stone. These diamonds are an example of a brilliant cut and high grade." He looked up at me, and I could not help but think that his jeweler's loupe made him appear to be someone out of a sci-fi story.

"I am sorry to say, though," he let go of my hand, removing the loupe, "when I enlarged it, the inscription was lost."

"That's okay," I said with a smile. Some things are better not found.

Traffic is heavier than I planned getting to the pier to pick up Mom and Dad. They are waiting for me and wave with untroubled smiles and glowing suntans. Both of them talk at once about their trip and their stay in Victoria, Dad leaning over from the back seat to interject a comment over my mom's shoulder. At a stop sign when it is my turn, my mother suddenly grows very quiet. I forgot to take the ring off.

"That's a beautiful ring," she says flatly, her most dangerous voice.

I merge. "Grandma gave it to me. Can we talk about this when we get home?"

Well, great! I manage to spoil their homecoming. I hoped to surprise both of them with a clean house, laundry done, dishwasher empty, and lawn mowed and watered before laying the bombshell.

"I understand from Ryan that you had some uneasy times with Grandma."

"Just one incident, that's all. No big deal. She had a bad day. Don't we all?"

Dad unloads the suitcases once I park the car. "Whoa! Fran-tastic! The yard looks great!"

"Thanks, Popsicle. All those years working with Dean and Dusty paid off—I no longer leave divots when I edge." I look beseechingly at him. "Dad, there's more to this than the ring. I didn't want to spoil your first night home."

He squeezes my shoulder. "Go talk to her."

Mom is in the living room at the dining table. "Honey, thank you! You put a lot of time and effort in cleaning. I appreciate it."

"Mom, can we talk?"

"Yes, I think we better."

I scurry to my room, take the picture out of the metal box, and with box in hand, sit opposite my mother. "I made iced tea," as if that is the most important thing I have to say.

"I'll get us all some," says my father from the kitchen.

I jump into the topic of our conversation. "Grandma wasn't trying to bury food all those times. She was trying to un-bury a Mason jar with a key to this metal box, She asked me to dig it up, only it wasn't under the roses; it was in front beneath the rhody. She said she wanted me to have the ring—I had it re-sized because I know we wear the same ring size. I really think you should have it. It's an engagement ring, the jeweler says, a halo ruby engagement ring, with an oval-cut .51 natural ruby and genuine, high-quality diamonds, worth about $2,500." I stop my run-on to catch a breath.

My mother reaches over to take my hand and examine the ring. "Yes, it is stunning. But you should have it. After all, it is your birthstone, very fitting for a twenty-first birthday gift from Grandma."

I slide the picture out in the middle of the table.

Mom puts her hand over it. "I know what's in the box, Fran. Ryan and I are snoops, too."

Miffed, I snip, "Grandma gave me permission to open the box, Mom. She wanted me to give the contents to you."

"It doesn't matter what is in that box because it won't ever change that, for me, Isaac Karlson was my father, my dad, my daddy. And I thank God that I *never*, even in my horrible teen years, let him know I knew otherwise."

Oh, how I want to ask her if she knows more, knows what the truth is. But some things cannot be known, and life goes on anyway. I will never know; it will always be left a mystery in our life, and we never speak again of it.

I don't know if I would have asked Grandma if I had another chance to speak with her; she gets pneumonia and dies the next week.

Chapter 10

Grandma's memorial is held at the Episcopalian church that Uncle Ryan belongs to and where he is an alderman. He gives a short and surprisingly lyrical eulogy of Grandma. I listen dry-eyed, but my mother does not. I finally slip the box of tissues between us on the pew. The reception is catered by the ladies of the church. There are no friends of Grandma's; all her closest in their eighties like her preceded her in dying. I did not expect to see anyone but family and am thrilled to recognize Mrs. Wessenfeld, hunched over a cane, overly dressed for the occasion with crinkled makeup, in the crowd. I hurry over to her.

"My dear, my dear! Look at you, so grown up and pretty!" She clasps my hands, and I give her a gentle hug. "I am so sorry to hear about your grandmother's passing. Evelyn and I used to have our morning coffee on the deck and gossip. She was a wonderful person and a good friend." She laughs that marvelous laugh of hers.

I want to ask about her husband and whatever became of the dogs, those bully dogs that used to chase me to school every day. My mother had made me talk to Mr. Wessenfeld, and long story short, I got a job walking the dogs, met Dean on his paper route, and a had a new perspective on life. I figure Athos, Porthos, and Aramis are long gone to the dog park in heaven, but Mr. W., as I affectionately called him, had a heart attack way back when I was in junior high school and was on oxygen when he came home; two years later, he and Mrs. W. sold their house and moved to a retirement community in Kent. I went once to visit with my parents and Grandma but never made it back there to see them again.

"Are you still at that nice place in Kent?"

"Oh, gracious, no, Fran. After George died, March 11, 2002, I went to live with my sister, Helen, in Issaquah."

Oh, crap. I'm sure my mother told me George had died and they, with Grandma, had gone to his memorial. I am embarrassed by my thoughtlessness.

Mrs. W. is much too nice of a person to make any reference to my lack of civility. She continues, "Helen's husband passed several years before George, and she was all by herself in a big rambling rambler." She snorts a little laugh, leaning into me with a lowered voice. "George never liked her much, and I didn't get to spend much time with her. Now all I have is time to spend, and it's mostly with her."

I am not going to touch that subject; let sleeping dogs and the male chauvinist lie. "Come with me," I tell her. "I'll get you a cup of coffee while you talk with Mom and Dad." I take her free hand and guide her over to where my mother and father are standing talking with cousins.

"Oh, dear Fran, not coffee. Tea if you please. Sugar and milk."

Changes, changes in everyone's life. Time is the only immutable thing in our lives.

After everyone has left, and we are on the way home, my mom turns in her seat and speaks to me with a wistful note in her voice. "My, I thought Mrs. Wessenfeld has aged. I guess I hadn't thought of her being eighty-two. It was nice of her son to drive her today. And he's in his fifties!"

"She was Grandma's age? I always thought of her as so much older than anyone I knew! Mrs. W. said she and Grandma used to sit on the deck with a cup of coffee and talk about people, gardening, and irritating chin hairs."

My mother rubs her chin. "Yes, they are."

Even my dad laughs, and we were all in a wonderful moment together.

"I had planned on a special night out for your birthday, Fran. But, truthfully, would you mind if we did next week? I thought your dad and I would take you to Canlis."

"Next week would be perfect! I'll have my dinner with Dean and Marcus, and maybe Annie, too, will come to their house. She's a little too obsessed by her wedding plans."

"Well, it is a once-in-a-lifetime event. Better that she is going forward and not in the place she was not too long ago."

Annie meets me at my house, and we drive together to have dinner with Dean and Marcus. They have put up streamers and strung a glittered "Happy 21st Birthday Girl" banner in the dining room from wall to wall and make us wear party hats. Annie clicks picture after picture with her iPhone until I shoot her a look that makes her cease and desist.

"Look at this spread! Spring rolls and crab cakes for hors d'oeuvres. Marcus, did you do this all yourself?"

"Oh, no, Dean helped."

Dean hands me a glass of Asti Spumante. "Yes, I did everything he told me to do. I am quite good at taking orders."

I look from one to the other, hoping his comment is not an indication of domestic strife. But they are both smiling at each other.

"Oh, none for me," Annie waggles her fingers. "I have a low tolerance for alcohol. Besides, someone has to be sober to drive."

I look at Dean, and he looks at me; this is a different incarnation of Annie from the one we knew in a previous life in junior high and high school.

At one point during dinner, Annie excuses herself to go to the bathroom. I sigh and lean over to Dean. "I hope she's not sticking her finger down her throat. It'd be a terrible waste of the salmon a la hollandaise."

"I don't think so, Fran. She appears to be pretty much in control of herself these days."

I raise my glass, and Dean and Marcus pantomime clinking glasses, a silent toast to hope.

Annie has some of her dessert; I have all of mine. "Mmmm, this is delightful! Caramel flan and mangoes! I never gained the 'freshman fifteen,' but I may put it on tonight."

"Actually," Dean steeples his hands, leaning forward on his elbows, "a study done by Ohio State University showed the average student gains only two to three pounds in the first year."

"It's comforting to know I've put on maybe two pounds. Anyway, Marcus, thank you again for all your culinary efforts to make this evening perfect!"

With a tilt of his head and palm up, he says, "M'lady, it was a pleasure. Happy birthday," and comes over to kiss me on the cheek. They all sing the birthday song, and Annie is right; no one can carry a tune.

Annie pops up from her seat, and a horrifying thought runs through my head that she is going to run off to the bathroom again. But she picks up plates and flatware instead. "Marcus, let me help clean up. I'd really like to do that."

Oh, Annie! We discussed how fastidious Marcus is, especially about the right way to do this or that in the kitchen. Actually, I said "peculiar," and she corrected me that he was "particular."

I might say his smile is a little strained, but his voice does not betray any stress.

"I'd be delighted to have your company in my kitchen. You can tell me, I hope, the name of a good wedding caterer. Let me show you how I load the dishwasher."

Dean pours me a second glass of champagne. "Well, that's a new one."

"Let's see how long it lasts before the fur flies." I tip my glass and feel the warmth of friendship and alcohol. "She has at least a dozen caterers he can choose from, with all the details no one should know."

Dean puts his glass down carefully. "That's a gorgeous ring your grandmother gave you. I'm glad you're wearing it on your right hand."

"Yes, it is sparkly, isn't it? Funny, you're not the first person to mention my wearing it on my right hand. No worries about me getting engaged anytime soon."

"Fran, promise me something. When you find your right mate, don't change for him. So many people try to be an ideal, or get an ideal person, that they stop being true to themselves, you know, as Dusty did for Frank. It's not only Dusty, but I see it in a lot of relationships. It never works out."

I chuckle. "Good advice, Dr. Dean. Soon you will probably have your own talk show or reality show, and I can be your first guest."

He slides a blue velvet box towards me. "The terms and conditions for you birthday, my friend."

I take the necklace out, stroking the dove with my thumb. "This is beautiful. For more than aesthetic reasons. I appreciate what these precious stones mean." I dangle it, the jewels winking. "Great symbolism." I twirl it, light refracting into rainbows. "The ruby, the oldest symbol of passion and commitment, is red, the color of love. The diamond—forever. The gentle dove, a symbol of the link between heaven and earth. Flowers and dove—Fran and Dean." I kiss his cheek softly and hand the necklace to him. "Put it on me?"

He squeezes my hand as he takes the necklace. When he has clasped it around my neck, he bends and kisses the nape of my neck. "Forever and a day," he whispers.

And this time, the chain lies cool against my skin. "I shall wear it to every wedding I go to: yours, Annie's, and mine." I reach for and take his hand for a perfect moment, one that I will always remember as the best of all birthdays.

Chapter 11

Adult isn't a noun, it's a verb.

— Kelly Williams Brown,
Adulting: How to Become a Grown-up in 468 Easy (ish) Steps

Annie gets married in her size-ten, more like a size-nine-and-a-half, wedding dress and has a big gala event on a snowless evening. Dean and Marcus are married in their home, catered by someone Annie recommended highly but didn't use for her own wedding. Annie goes on to graduate with a post graduate degree and become a well-known expert in eating disorders, traveling all over the world to give speeches at conferences. She is a terrific speaker.

I graduate and land a plum teaching position at City University of Seattle. I have a small studio apartment downtown and on a cool November evening literally have a run-in with my future husband while pulling into the parking garage as he is backing out of his space. Furious, I stand glaring at him, pointing to the dent in the door of my new Prius. He squats down, looking intently at it, and then smiles at me. "It really won't affect the aerodynamics."

I snarl. "It will be fixed."

He cocks an eyebrow. "Certainly. A minor intention, er, indentation."

With this exchange come other offers of dinners, movies, and a hike to Cedar Falls in the North Cascades where Aaron proposes. When I am five months pregnant, we buy a starter house within walking distance of where my mom and dad live.

"What's your latest project, Mother? As if I don't know." I scrunch myself down onto the chair at my place at the kitchen island.

"A baby quilt," she intones with a smile that would light up New York.

"Well, I'm sure she'll just love it," I reply with a matching smile.

"A girl! Any names yet?"

My goodness, is she really doing her happy dance? "Mother, you're going to wear yourself out. I've got four months to go." I sip my cranberry juice. "What do you think of Tinker? Kind of catchy with the last name of Bell, don't you think?"

She looks stricken and then tries to recover. "Tinker. She'll love you for that."

"Maybe just call her Baby? That was Aaron's idea."

She looks truly distressed.

I laugh and shake my head. "Seriously, I like Zoey. Short and sweet."

That brings back her smile until she answers the phone. "It's for you. Frank Freeman."

"Fran, this is Frank. Freeman."

"Yes?" I try to sound detached. I let him do all the talking.

"Fran! I'm calling because I need to make amends, and I want you to know that I have been clean and sober for two years. I'm married with a family, and I want to let Elizabeth know that I've really changed, you know? I want to see my son. I want to get hold of her."

"Frank, I don't know where she is. I have not seen or heard from her since that last time in the hospital, when she lost her baby girl." Instinctively, I put my hand over my baby bump.

"Fran, I know it was an awful thing. I live with regrets. I want to tell her how sorry I am I hurt her."

"Frank, what you did to Dusty hurt us all. Her friends—Annie, Dean, me."

"Well, like I care about that . . . guy."

Like I care about you, Frankenstein? "In the unlikely event that I should see her, I'll tell her you called and left information in case she wants to talk to you. But, Frank, don't hold your breath." I hang up, thinking that maybe he should hold his breath.

I should have asked my mother for a catcher's mitt to take the curve ball that comes later that day.

While I am browsing in the UW bookstore for supplies for my upcoming classes, I happen to glance up to see a young woman close to me, so close I can see her dark eyes. She is talking to a salesperson when a young brown-haired boy, nine or ten years old, goes up to her, "Mom! Mom!" chattering excitedly. Calmly, she lays her hand on top of his head, finishes her discussion with the clerk, and turns to her boy, her baby bump obvious.

I stand staring at her. No, it cannot be Dusty. This woman has dark, cropped, straight hair, and brown eyes. She is muscular and has what appears to be a very bad burn on her arm. But as blood calls to blood, bonded by love, and you just know you know, I know it is Dusty. She recognizes me the moment I say her name.

"Fran! It *is* you!"

The hug is awkward, both of our baby bumps, well, bumping, but we manage to get our arms around each other. "What? Where have you been? Oh, my, what now?"

We walk to a nearby restaurant. And so we talk over lunch, poor not-William-any-longer is bored to fidgets. Dusty, now Juliet, and William, now Teddy, went underground that day she left her mother's, courtesy of a woman's network for abused women and children.

"And, Fran, I went to college, Central Washington University in Ellensburg, and got my degree in fine arts. You know," she looks at me sheepishly, "I would discuss ideas and projects with you, as if you were my imaginary friend sitting beside me. Thank God, Fran, you are not imaginary!" Like quick-fire, she changes the subject. "In fact," she leans back in her chair and laughs, "I earned my tuition by painting. House painting!"

"Well, you've obviously done a lot more than that, Dusty." I point to her belly and her arm.

"Yes, and Richard is wonderful. This," she holds her arm up, "is from a careless act of welding. I do metal sculpture, and what can I say? I got distracted and paid for it." Her eyes light up, and even her words have a smile in them. "I actually sold the last piece, *Holding onto Faith,* a bronze sculpture of Atlas. I sold it to a private collector." She looks pointedly at me. "I have to say that my faith paid off!"

Teddy interrupts by blurting out, "Mommy! Why does she call you Dusty? Your name's Juliet."

"Because, sweetheart, that was my nickname when I first met Fran. We've been friends for a long time." She leans close to her son and rubs noses with him. "Longer than ten years."

"Why Juliet?" I could never think of Frankenstein as Romeo.

"Tragic heroine. Elsa seemed too obvious. And I needed to be reminded that blind romanticism can be costly."

I put down my napkin and push away my plate. "Frank called me. He wanted information about you." I take a sip of water. "Of course, I had none."

She leans over and lowers her voice. "I'm not surprised. He's contacted everyone in my previous life."

"But you do have an order of protection, right?"

"It's only a piece of paper. There's no magic in it." She touches her shoulder to mine, laying her hand over mine. "Fran, I know that it is hard to understand, but I do not hate Frank. Oh, I did for a long time," she removes her hand and roots in her purse for a handful of coupons that she gives to Teddy, "Sort these by color, sweetheart," with an aside to me, "I'm queen of coupons."

With Teddy distracted, she continues, "Fran, I was so lonely, so alone. But," she sits back and carefully considers her words, "I had plenty of time to think about how my life had been like a see-saw. I'd just been sitting on one end of the teeter-totter, letting events be the heavier weight on the other end. Looking at my situation from another perspective, I had been given a chance to change from being someone who always reacted to being someone who is a strong person in her own right. We all have choices, and I have made some bad ones. But isn't it all about the learning? Finding our way? Although some of us," she sighs, "have a steeper learning curve than others."

This woman sitting beside me definitely has a sense of self, I think. The strength to let go, forgive, and go on with her life on her terms. "You once said you envied me, Dusty. Now I have to say I admire you. You've come out the other side a whole person, able to forgive and be loving. I don't know that I would have been able to do that."

We have a brief moment between us of silence, but it feels as if we are retying the broken ribbons of our friendship.

"Mom! Look! I got them all done!"

Dusty smiles at her son and then tries swiping at Teddy's mouth for the spot of jelly. "Fran, I have to run. Do you remember where my father's house is? Can you come by tomorrow?"

I nod. "I'm free after ten."

"Meet me there at eleven." She hugs me. I hug her again before she gathers her purse and purchases and hustles herself and Teddy out to her car.

The next morning is balmy with high clouds scudding across sunny, blue skies. It seems birds are everywhere, twittering loudly in the oak tree in the front of the Connors' house. Different paint on the outside, but still the same immaculate green lawn. I pull up to park at the curb in time to see Teddy bolt from Dusty's car. Teddy runs to Sylvia, who does not look any worse for wear after all this time, and throw himself into her arms. Dusty waits for a few minutes and then embraces Sylvia. I sit there in my car, seeing this and wondering what else do I not understand; how many worlds do we exist in simultaneously?

I tuck the envelope with money that was to be given to Dusty that Sylvia gave me so very long ago deep into my purse and approach the happy group on the lawn. Sylvia smiles warmly at me, offering her open arms for a welcoming hug. "Oh, my, it is so good to see you! Come in, come in! Let's have coffee. Or tea. Whatever you ladies would like."

I turn to Dusty; her eyes are green again. "You're looking more like your former self! Except for the hair."

"Contacts, and I am so glad to be rid of them!" She touches her hair. "It's going to be ugly, but I'll be so happy to have my color and curls back!" She laughs with sparkling eyes and dimples. "To think that I used to want straight hair!"

Once inside the house, the air filled with delicious scent of chocolate, I turn to Sylvia. "I think I owe you an apology. I thought you didn't care. I never figured it out." I take out the envelope with the fifteen hundred dollars in it and hand it to her. "I guess if you want, you can give it to her yourself."

"Oh, Fran, I never expected it back. But I'm not surprised." She leans over and gives me a quick peck on the cheek. "I so wanted to tell you, but you do understand that no one, not even Elizabeth's father, knew that I had anything to do with it. That's why we call it an underground operation." She flicks the envelope on my shoulder as she heads for the kitchen.

Sylvia's daughter, Sophia, dressed in jeans and a black-and-white t shirt with "#1 Aunt" printed in glitter on it, comes out of her bedroom into the living room. She motions to Teddy to come beside her and hugs him. "Hi ya, Teddy Bear. Want to help me make some more chocolate chip cookies?"

"You betcha!" Teddy grabs Sophia's hand and pulls her along into the kitchen.

Dusty and I move to the couch, and I turn to her. "But how can you be sure it's safe to come out from hiding? Frank could show up, and what if he went ballistic?"

"I'm told he's in Michigan and remarried. You said he said he was clean and sober. It's a chance, a chance I'm willing to take."

"He hasn't changed, though, Dusty. Believe me."

"But I have." She locks eyes with me. "I won't be with him alone, and I won't argue with him. Believe me, I've thought this through. And if I know Frank, he'll want to see Teddy for a time or two, and then he'll fade away. Christmas, birthdays, are not something he will remember." She looks from to Sylvia to Teddy and back to me. "I have to get my life back. It's time."

And fortunately for all of us, she is right. Frank makes a grand show of the reformed father with presents for his son and flowers for Dusty when he comes to her father's house. He stays a week at a nearby hotel but, after all the promises, never contacts Teddy or Dusty again.

I have a newer photograph beside the older ones on my desk that my husband took at one of our backyard parties. When I pick it up and look at it, I am reminded of that perfect summer day before time would unravel the threads of our relationships. In the background of the photo are my mother and father, my mother burping my baby girl, Zoey; Teddy behind my mother's shoulder peering intently at her; Sylvia cradling Dusty's daughter, Theia—named after the Titan goddess who birthed Helios, the sun, Selene, the moon, and Eos, dawn; Sophia holding Theia's tiny hand; Jon, Richard, Mr. Connor, and Marcus beside them. In the forefront, I am on the outside, then Dusty, and Annie; Dean is behind us with his arms splayed across our shoulders, his head resting on my left shoulder. We are all in t-shirts and shorts and similar sandals—I am the only one wearing a necklace that reflects the light in a starburst. We are all smiling, the four of us together, as if we have not a care in the world, captured in that twinkling forever.